DELAYED DEPARTURE

TALL PAUL

Author's Tranquility Press
ATLANTA, GEORGIA

Copyright © 2024 by Tall Paul

All rights reserved. No part of this publication may be reproduced, distributed or transmitted in any form or by any means, including photocopying, recording, or other electronic or mechanical methods, without the prior written permission of the publisher, except in the case of brief quotations embodied in critical reviews and certain other noncommercial uses permitted by copyright law. For permission requests, write to the publisher, addressed "Attention: Permissions Coordinator," at the address below.

Tall Paul/Author's Tranquility Press
3900 N Commerce Dr. Suite 300 #1255
Atlanta, GA 30344
www.authorstranquilitypress.com

Ordering Information:
Quantity sales. Special discounts are available on quantity purchases by corporations, associations, and others. For details, contact the "Special Sales Department" at the address above.

Delayed Departure/Tall Paul
Paperback: 978-1-964037-40-0
eBook: 978-1-964037-06-6

AUTHOR'S NOTE
♠ ♣ ♥ ♦

Delayed Departure was solely inspired by the printing of Frederic Remington's pen-and-ink drawing, *They Left Him Thar in the Trail,* on a T-shirt that my good friend Robert Bruce Miller wore to work one day. The very minute I saw it, my mind began thinking about writing a book based on that print. I was engaged in writing another book at the time, *Nothin' but Try: The Shane Drury Story*, but I wanted to keep the image on the T-shirt in the back of my mind until I had time to start writing about it.

At the time, I was working for Mr. Miller, a prominent Boulder, Colorado, attorney, as an investigator/paralegal. I told my boss that he had two options. He could either take off the shirt and make me a photocopy, or he could lay on the copier, but either way I had to have a picture of that shirt. At first, he thought I was joking, but the more we talked, the more he realized I was serious and took off the shirt and made me a copy of the picture.

After Mr. Miller received his copy of the book *Delayed Departure*, he mailed me the T-shirt. However, according to a note included with the shirt, my retaining the shirt was conditional upon his getting an acceptable part in the movie.

CONTENTS

AUTHOR'S NOTE i
ACKNOWLEDGEMENTS iii
PREFACE v

CHAPTER 1 THE HOMECOMING 1
CHAPTER 2 LIFE 14
CHAPTER 3 LIFE CHANGES 20
CHAPTER 4 HEADING WEST 27
CHAPTER 5 RIDDLE SOLVED 36
CHAPTER 6 RANCH LIFE 44
CHAPTER 7 TOUGH DECISIONS 53
CHAPTER 8 THE WAR 58
CHAPTER 9 CAPTURED 64
CHAPTER 10 RECOVERY 68
CHAPTER 11 RESCUED 73
CHAPTER 12 REMEMBERING 78
CHAPTER 13 WHITEHOUSE PLAN 87
CHAPTER 14 COMMENCE OPERATIONS 94

ACKNOWLEDGEMENTS

I would like to thank Robert Bruce Miller for his support during my writing of both books, *Nothin' but Try* and *Delayed Departure*.

As many of you know, I live off grid in the mountains of northwest Colorado. I title myself as a mountain man and author. Where I live, there are other cabins that are mostly used as summer vacation cabins or hunting cabins. I used the names of several of my friends who own cabins in the vicinity, and I would like to thank all of them for allowing me to use their names as characters in *Delayed Departure*.

PREFACE

This story, although fiction, is based on actual historic events. It begins during WWI, which began in 1914, and travels through a span of time, ending with the assassination of the president of the United States in 1963.

There will be mention of things such as the famous Hole in the Wall, the outlaw hideout of Butch Cassidy and the Wild Bunch.

The orphan train, which transported approximately two hundred thousand children from cities such as New York City to places in America's Midwest for adoption, ran between 1854 until 1929 and plays a part in bringing the main character to the west.

The events leading up to and during World War II are, although taken out of context, important factors in bringing the main character to light. Events such as Japan's attempt to invade mainland Australia, Japan's release of some nine thousand (9,000) bombs attached to balloons and launched into the jet stream, with approximately one thousand (1,000) reaching North America, of which a mere three hundred (300) landed in the United States, the attack on Pearl Harbor, and other historical events all come together to create this story.

CHAPTER 1

THE HOMECOMING

November 1918

The Great War is over, and the Germans are defeated. It was a bittersweet time. Men were returning from war to a hero's welcome, but for some, the real heroes were those who would not be coming home.

Wil Drury and many of his fellow soldiers are heading back home to return to their former lives. They receive a tumultuous welcome as they land in the New York harbor and are paraded through the streets of New York City. Confetti is dropped from the rooftops as the cavalcade of waving soldiers goes by. The crowd roars their congratulations and "welcome home" to the passing troops. In return, the soldiers toss candy, money, anything they have to spare, to the cheering crowd.

Wil is packed in one of the many buses taking the soldiers through the cheering streets. Although his heart is torn from the loss of his brother, he too is caught up in the joy of the moment. He too is compelled to toss trinkets to the crowd. His duffel is packed away in the bus storage area, and he cannot retrieve any tokens to throw to the crowd. He searches his pockets, hoping to find something that he can toss to the crowd, but the only thing he can come up with is a deck of cards. Leaning out of one of the bus windows, he opens the deck and begins tossing the cards one by one. In an instant, just as he is tossing a card, he sees in the crowd a young lady, most definitely of European descent. It seems as if time stands still as his eyes fixate on her. He has tossed a card, which seems like it will fall at her feet, but it seems, momentarily, to have stopped in midair.

Wil cannot help but stare at her. He nearly falls out of the bus window stretching to get a better look at her. The sunlight and the cool breeze caress her wealth of auburn hair as she stands with her hand held against her belly, caressing the child she has conceived. Wil watches as she reaches down to pick up the card he has thrown. For that second, she disappears from his sight, but he sees her again as she stands back upright with the card in her hand. She looks at the card, the queen of diamonds, smiles, and holds the card against her unborn child, then quickly turns to look at the bus. Her eyes catch the eyes of the soldier that threw the card. Their eyes are locked in that short moment in time, as if she was staring at someone, she thought she knew. The bus continues down the street, and she slowly disappears from Wil's sight and he from hers. For that single moment, Wil felt an attraction to that woman, but he was confused as to why. He didn't know her, and he is heading back home to marry his sweetheart, but somehow, he felt a sense of affection for her. Spontaneously he begins to rub his shirt pocket that contains Tall's pocketknife.

Finished touring the town, the buses pulled into the depot, and the soldiers disembarked and gathered their gear. They bid each other adieu. "We'll keep in touch," they assure each other with a firm handshake and a pat on the shoulder. With that, they each head in separate directions to their final destinations—home.

Wil is headed to Wyoming, back to the ranch that his ancestors had homesteaded. It is a great spread, rich in Wyoming history. On the bus headed back home, Wil ponders his feelings for the woman on the street. Unknowingly, he reaches into his pocket, takes out Tall's knife, and begins to rub it. Wil is restless on the long bus ride home and drifts in and out of sleep. From time to time, distantly, he stares out the window, and his mind drifts off to memories of Tall.

The room is dimly lit, and Wil says to Tall, "You know, Tall, when we get in the action, one of us could get killed or captured."

"You are not going to get killed or captured, little brother. I will see to that," Tall responds sternly.

"Well," Wil replies, "I was just thinking that maybe we should exchange something, you know, just in case."

"And just what were you thinking we should exchange?" Tall questions.

We don't have much," Wil suggests, "but perhaps we should exchange the knives that Grandpa Maxie made for us."

"You know," Tall says, "that's not a bad idea. They have our names on them, and if something were to happen to one of us, then the other could take that back home as a remembrance. I would want mine to go to my firstborn."

"I didn't know you had a firstborn, Tall," Wil replies.

"Well, the war ain't over yet," responds Tall jokingly. "I've been seeing this little gal in town, and she's a real keeper. I told her if she can get to the States after the war that she should come to Wyoming and look me up."

"And does this little gal have a name?" Wil asks.

"Let's just say I will have a fond *memory* of this one," Tall quips.

"I don't know why you always have to talk in riddles, Tall," Wil responds.

The two brothers exchange knives and continue talking, with Tall ignoring Wil's last comment.

"You know, Wil," Tall continues, "I've lived a pretty good life."

Wil responds, "What are you talking about, Tall? You're not even thirty years old yet."

"Oh hell, Wil," Tall replies, "it ain't about years. It's about livin'. Just think back to all the good times we had back on the ranch."

Wil's mind drifts off to a time when a young Wil and Tall are caught in a rainstorm while out fishing; they have their dog (Jake) with them, as it is impossible to leave the ranch without him. They take shelter in a small cave on the hillside. As the lightning strikes, lighting up the blackened sky, they huddle together all soaking wet, the dog, Tall, and Wil. Suddenly Tall turns to Wil and says,

"This reminds me of the poem that Uncle Kermit used to like, 'High up in the lonely mountains, the Indians watched and waved. The wolves in the forest, the bears in the bushes and I in my path belated. There we two in the stormy dark, I and the wolf together, side by side through the long, long night, we hid from the awful weather. His wet fur pressed against me, each of us warmed the other, each of us felt in the stormy dark that man and beast were brother."

"Seems like you had a poem for every occasion," Wil remembers.

"I don't know where you always came up with that stuff."

"Just lucky, I guess," Tall responds.

"Well, you certainly must have a poem for this occasion, don't you, Tall?" Wil asks.

Tall responds as he fumbles around in his pack, "I just happen to have one here that I just wrote."

"You mean you don't have it memorized?" Wil chuckles.

"Nope," Tall replies with a grin. "There's not been enough time for that yet." Tall hands Wil the folded-up piece of paper he has taken from his pack.

"Here ya go, Wil," Tall says.

"You mean you ain't even gonna read it to me?" Wil queries.

"Somehow, Wil, I always thought you knew how to read. Guess I should have known better. Here, give it back and I'll read it to you, but you probably won't understand it, and I'm not gonna explain it to you," Tall states jokingly.

Wil hands Tall the poem. Tall unfolds it, pulls the lamp closer, and reads to Wil.

It's Me

At first, I thought little about him,
Though I knew that look in his eye.
A stranger, but somehow, I knew him,
I was sure from days long gone by.

I lingered a bit when I saw him.
His look took me back years in time.
I thought 'bout the ways that I knew him.
I had memories, some sad, some just fine.

In truth, I knew all 'bout this person.
There were things that no one else knew.
Some things that should be kept secret;
Some secrets that were told to a few.

I remembered this man kind and gentle.
I recalled his rage like some beast.
Some things I wanted to recall,
Others, to remember the least.

Yes, I knew all about him,
Like a God who keeps tabs on one's life.
I knew of his good deeds and bad ones,
Of his happiness, troubles, and strife.

As I knelt by the tarn and saw him,
In the water's reflection I could see.

I said to myself staring at him,
Of course, I should know
him…it's me!

"Wow," Wil states, "that's pretty deep, Tall."

Tall folds the poem back up and places it into his pocket without saying a word.

In the silence, Wil's mind again drifts off to memories of Tall. Wil recalls the time he and Tall were out on horseback checking cattle. It was a beautiful, sunny, summer day with a rich blue Wyoming sky free of clouds. Everything was going along smoothly and lazily when all of a sudden, Tall sees a bobcat in the distance. With a whoop and a holler, Tall grabs his rope and spurs his horse, racing after the surprised cat. The cat takes off for the creek bottom, racing through the brush and trees to escape the oncoming danger. Tall, hot on the heels of the bobcat, has the brush and tree limbs tearing at his clothes as he refuses to stop the pursuit. He eventually makes a valiant attempt to rope the fleeing bobcat, but all is in vain as he is knocked from his horse by a low tree branch that he is unable to avoid. Wil gathers Tall's horse and brings him back. Tall, bruised up, clothes torn, and a little bloody, is laughing as he gathers himself. "Did you see that, Wil?" Tall asks.

"I almost had him." Will replies.

"And just what were you going to do if you caught him?"

"Not too sure about that, Wil, but we would have figured out something," Tall answers back.

Handing Tall the reins of his horse, Wil mumbles, "Yeah, I guess we would have thought of something. Perhaps *we* should think of something that will keep Mom from getting upset about your clothes."

"Yeah." Tall chuckles. "Guess you can work on that on the ride home."

"Why am I the one who always has to explain it to Mom?" Wil mumbles to himself.

Wil mumbles this to himself over and over and suddenly wakes to find himself on the bus going home. He is still gripping Tall's knife, and he opens it to look at Tall's name on it, then closes it. Staring out the bus window, Wil again drifts off to sleep, and his mind fades again to memories with Tall.

Wil recalls the time that he and Tall were out mending a fence. "We best be heading back for lunch," Tall commands.

Wil agrees, and they load the tools into the bed of the truck and head for home. Wil is driving, and just as they get started back, Tall sees a badger running up the road.

"Stay after him," Tall barks as he slips out the truck window into the back of the pickup.

Tall grabs the digging bar and holds it like a spear as Wil races the truck toward the badger. The badger, sensing the hot pursuit, stops suddenly, and Will runs the truck right over top of him. The badger is quicker than Wil and darts out from under the truck, heading back down the road in the opposite direction.

"Put 'er in reverse," Tall hollers.

Wil does as Tall requests, and Tall takes up position at the back of the truck bed. Wil is racing in reverse and catches up to the badger, but again the badger stops. Wil is not going to let the badger outfox him this time, so he slams on the brakes. Tall is in throwing position, holding the digging bar like a spear, and as Wil brakes, Tall is thrown out of the back of the truck and lays on the ground face-to-face with the badger. Wil is frozen in the truck, fearing that he has really screwed up this time and perhaps even run over his brother. He sits quietly for what seems like an eternity and catches a glimpse as the badger runs out through the sagebrush. Wil is relieved to hear Tall laughing. He takes a deep breath and exits the truck, only to see Tall lying on the ground, halfway under the truck with the "spear" still in his hand.

"I thought I killed you for sure, or at least crippled you, and the badger was going to eat you," Wil remarks to Tall, who was still laughing.

"Well," Tall quips as he crawls out from under the truck and dusts himself off, "it sure took you long enough to check on me. You should have seen the look on that badger's face when I landed on the ground under that truck. He was scared to death."

"Probably so," Wil replies, "and so was I. I guess this is going to be the topic of the dinner table today."

"Pretty exciting, you have to admit," Tall responds. "Damn, that was funny!"

With that, they load back into the cab of the truck and head for home, Tall still chuckling about the whole incident.

Wil's mind is now back in the room with Tall and breaking the silence, Wil remarks, "You always were the one to take chances, Tall."

"Oh hell, Wil, that's exactly what I'm talking about when I say I've lived a pretty good life," Tall counters.

"You know, Wil, it wouldn't hurt if you did some things different now and then."

"Yeah, like what?" Wil questions.

"I'm glad you asked, Wil," Tall responds. "I been looking through these dime novels that I bought."

Wil interrupts, "Just why did you buy them anyway? You already know all those stories."

"Now, Wil," Tall snaps, "what have I told you about interrupting me when I'm on a roll? I'm not sure what I'll do with them, but this one I want you to have."

Oh, well, pardon me," Wil responds humbly.

"Okay," Tall quips. "Now what I was about to say was that you should grow a mustache like this one here that Wyatt Earp has." Tall hands Wil the book with Wyatt Earp on the cover with his full mustache.

Wil questions, "Now why would I want to have something like that draped all over my beautiful face, and what would Carla think?"

"Damn it, Wil," Tall snaps. "What does it matter what other people think? It's about you, not about what other people think. You put too much stock in what other people think. Wouldn't you want to do something for you and not care about what other people think?"

"I'm not sure I even want to have a mustache like that regardless of what other people think," Wil responds. "I'm just really not too sure I would like a huge mustache like that."

"Well," Tall replies, "you will never know unless you give it a try, and I would sure like to see how you look. So there, if you want to please someone besides yourself, you could just do it as a favor to me after the war."

"Okay, Tall, okay," Wil answers, laying the book on the stand beside his bed. "After the war, I'll give it a thought." Wil continues to mumble to himself, "I'll give it a thought, I'll give it a thought..." and again wakes to find himself on the bus ride home. He takes his hand and rubs his face as if he were sporting that huge Earp mustache, grins, looks out the bus window, and fades back to sleep. Wil's mind again drifts off to memories of Tall.

Wil and Tall are sitting in silence, contemplating the next day's adventure.

The silence is broken by Tall, who states, "It's getting late. We better get going. We will need to be in position before light."

Wil recalls Tall reaching over and blowing out the lamp, and then the two are on the battlefield engaged in a great firefight with the enemy. Tall and Wil are hidden and begin sniping at enemy troops as they come into range. Wil's position is compromised, and suddenly he is hit by enemy fire.

Wil reaches for his radio and calls Tall. "Tall, over," Wil speaks into the radio. "Come on, Tall, answer, damn it!"

"I'm a little busy here, Wil. What is it?" Tall radios back.

"I'm hit, Tall. My shoulder is broken, and I can't shoot anymore. They hit me in my gun shoulder," Wil exclaims.

"Well, get the hell out of there!" Tall responds.

"They're closing in on me, Tall. I don't think I can get away," Wil radios back.

"Wil, you've had a broken shoulder before, and it never affected your legs. Now get the hell going, and I'll keep them off your ass just like I did all those bulls!" Tall replies sternly.

"Tall, you have got to come too. They will discover your position once you start covering for me, so come on and go with me," Wil begs.

"Wil, there is no time for bullshit, now get going, and I'll be right behind once you are in the clear," Tall demands.

With hesitation, Wil vacates his post while Tall lays down cover, but just as Wil feared, Tall's position was now compromised also. Tall refuses to stop firing in order to give Wil cover to get away, and just as Wil is in the clear and begins to radio Tall, there is a loud explosion near Tall's location.

Wil screams into the radio, "Tall, Tall, Tall!" but there is no answer. Tall's position has been hit, and Wil awakens while mumbling, "Tall, Tall, Tall."

Startled, he looks around at his whereabouts, and realizing he is still on the bus headed home, he stares out the bus window. At that moment, in the darkness just before dawn, he sees a vision of the woman who picked up the playing card he threw from the bus in New York. As the sun breaks over the horizon, her image fades away. Wil can no longer go back to sleep, and he realizes that he is back in Wyoming.

Wil becomes impatient to get home as he looks out the window at the antelope racing across the open prairie. The bus pulls into the Kaycee country store. Wil gets off the bus, retrieves his baggage, sets it down on the porch, and walks into the store.

Sitting in a chair sipping coffee is Roger Cappi, a longtime friend of the Drury family. Roger is a big, burly man with a full beard and looks more like a lumberjack than a rancher. Joining him is the store owner, Darrell Snow. Joanne is busy behind the counter. Darrell has his back to the door, but Roger always keeps his eye on the door and notices Wil as he walks in.

"I heard you were coming home," Roger states in his rough voice, startling Wil.

"Roger. Darrell? How have you all been?" Wil questions. "And, Joanne, how are things with you?"

"How you getting along, son?" Roger asks.

"I guess I'm okay. I made it through the war," Wil states sheepishly. "I was kinda hoping I could catch a ride back to the homestead."

"Well now, how about that, Wil," Roger begins. "It's your lucky day 'cause I just happen to be going that way."

"I thought for sure you told me you were heading for Casper today, Roger," Darrell remarks.

"Now, Darrell," Roger steps in, "what would I possibly want to go to Casper for? Where did you ever get an idea like that?"

Joanne looks over at Roger and smiles, knowing full well that Roger was going to Casper, but has changed his mind to give Wil a ride home.

"Not sure why I thought that, Roger," Darrell ponders and looks over at Joanne with a smile.

Wil promised Roger's sister Carla that he would marry her if he made it home from the war. Wil and Carla were high school sweethearts. Wil opens up, "How is Carla doing, Roger?"

"Well, it sure took you long enough to ask," Roger snaps back jokingly. "She's still waiting for you, if that's what you're asking. I told her she was foolish to do so."

Wil just smiles and nods his head.

"And you can bet she'd have been here had she known you were gonna get here today," Roger continues. "She'll sure be happy to know that you're back home."

"I gotta get home before I see her, Roger," Wil states with hesitance, "but if you let her know I'm back, I'll sure come visit her tomorrow."

"Oh, I'll let her know all right," Roger states firmly. "If I didn't, it would be my head, and you know that, Wil Drury. She's a strong-willed woman, and all I can say is good luck to both of you."

With that, Roger takes one last sip of coffee, bids Joanne and Darrell good day with a tip of his hat and heads out the door to his pickup with Wil.

"Good to see you guys," Wil says as he leaves with Roger.

Roger and Wil head toward the Hole in the Wall. The trip is long and dusty. Very little is said as Roger drives on, and Wil looks out the window.

"You know, Wil," Roger breaks the silence, "if you ever want to talk about it, I'm here for you, my friend. War is a terrible thing, especially when we lose the ones, we're closest to. Sometimes it helps a little to talk about it. I know how close you and Tall were."

"Thanks, Roge," Wil replies, shortening Roger's name, "not just yet, but maybe someday. I always knew you would be there for me. You're a great friend."

The pickup is getting close to the Hole in the Wall, and Wil says, "Hey, Roge, let me out here and I'll walk the rest of the way. I'd like to take that shortcut through the hole."

"Say what?" Roger questions. "It's still quite a way to your place, even taking the shortcut."

"I know," Wil replies, "but I just want a little more time to think before I see the folks."

"Whatever you want, buddy," Roger agrees and pulls the truck over to let Wil out.

Wil gets out of the pickup and grabs his duffel from the back, but Roger says, "Hey, Wil, why don't you let me drop that bag off at your place? I'm going right by there, and there's no need for you to lug that any farther than you already have, and I can let your folks know you're on your way, if you want."

"Thanks, Roge," Wil replies, "I guess that would lighten my load just a bit. My guess is that when you drop off my bag, the folks will know I'm coming. I'll be seeing you around. Thanks again." And with that being said, Wil turns and starts walking as Roger, shaking his head, watches him walk toward the Hole in the Wall and slowly out of sight.

As Roger sits, an idea suddenly comes to him. He smiles and talks to himself, "I guess Wil wouldn't mind if we had a little homecoming party for him. Might even help him deal with things some." Roger puts the truck in reverse, turns around, and heads back to Kaycee to grab some party supplies, pick up Carla, and then head to Wil's homestead.

Wil walks slowly as he is making his way home. Looking carefully at the countryside as he walks along and pondering things, he and Tall had done. Wil talks to himself but is actually talking to Tall as he walks along and points out the places where he and Tall hunted, shot deer, bear, elk, bobcats, coyotes, and mountain lions.

It is nearly sunset as Wil reaches the old ranch house. He pauses and takes in a deep breath before making his way down the hill to the cemetery. He stops at the little cemetery with its faded white picket fence and breathes a sigh of relief to see that there are no new graves, just the old ones and a small wooden cross bearing Tall's name. He whispers to himself, "Well, Tall, I guess you and Daddy will be gettin' to spend some time together now."

His mother looks out the window and sees him at the graves. She knows that Wil is hurting with the kind of hurt that even a mother cannot cure. She holds her hand to her face and turns away to let the guests know that Wil has arrived and will be there soon. She is comforted by her mother, Jackie. Maxie and Roger are talking quietly while Carla stares out the window.

   Wil turns, walks to the house, and is greeted as he walks through the door. He gives his mother and grandmother a hug, shakes hands with Grandpa Maxie and Roger, then turns to Carla. She rushes to him with teary eyes, and they embrace passionately.

CHAPTER 2

♠ ♣ ♥ ♦

LIFE

Wil stays busy breaking back into life as a rancher. He never speaks of his brother Tall, although he visits the graveyard every day.

Wil's mother, grandmother Jackie, and Carla are all busy planning the wedding while Wil and Maxie are busy puttering around in the shop. Wil begins to fumble around, looking for a knife to cut some twine.

"What the devil are you looking for, Wil?" Maxie asks.

"A knife," Wil replies with a bit of an embarrassed tone.

"Well, here," Maxie says, reaching into his pocket and pulling out his knife, "you can use mine. Guess you lost the one I made for you." Wil does not answer but takes Maxie's knife. "Well, I suppose I could make you another one without too much trouble," Maxie states. "That war took a lot of things from lots of people. Don't fret about it, Wil."

"Thanks, Gramps," Wil says as he hands Maxie back his knife without looking at him.

The wedding is held at the ranch and is a modest affair, with only a few close friends and relatives in attendance: Wil's mother, Maxie and Jackie, Carla's brother Roger, close friends and neighbors—Robert and Sandra Amis and the Kaycee storekeepers, Darrell and Joanne Snow. Roger does the honor of giving away his sister since both their parents have passed away. Wil does not have a best man, so Roger also gives the toast at the wedding supper. Tapping his glass to get everyone's attention and then raising it, Roger boldly begins, "I'd like to propose a toast to the newlyweds, my lovely sister Carla, who can never seem to make very good choices, and to ugly here, may you live a long prosperous life together and bear many children. I hope that each sunrise and sunset find you as deeply in love as you are today and that the years will never distance you."

Life gets back to the norm for Wil and Carla, although Wil has a lot of difficulty forgetting about Tall. Every day, right after breakfast, Wil visits the little cemetery and talks with Tall.

One day while cleaning out one of the rooms in the ranch house, Carla finds Wil's duffel bag that he brought home from the war. Wil has just entered the house, and Carla remarks to him, "Say, Wil, your duffel bag is in the room I have been cleaning out, and I wondered if you wanted me to do something with it."

"Yeah," Wil responds, "I've been meaning to get to that. I still have my rifle in there and some other things that I need to put away. I'll get to that this afternoon."

"Good," Carla says with a smile, "I want to get this room finished. I think it will make a good room for the baby."

"What?" Wil asks.

"Yes, Wil," Carla answers with a glow, "we are going to have a baby."

"Well, that's a hell of a way to tell me," Wil states, "but I'm very pleased. Are you sure? When did you find out?"

"Just yesterday, and yes, I'm very sure," Carla replies.

"Yesterday? And you are just now telling me? Okay then," Wil says, giving Carla a big hug, "I guess I'll get that bag out of there and get things in order. Yes, I'm very pleased indeed."

Wil grabs the duffel bag from the room and takes it out to the shop. The first thing he takes from the bag is the sniper rifle and several boxes of cartridges that he brought back from the war. Wil mumbles to himself, "Guess I'd better find a place for this somewhere out of sight." Wil takes the rifle into the house to one of the upstairs rooms. He opens the closet and removes a board from the back wall. Wil places the rifle and several boxes of cartridges in the hollow of the wall and replaces the board. "Should be safe there," Wil says to himself.

Returning to the rest of the duffel, Wil finds the Wyatt Earp dime novel and the poem that Tall put in his bag after he went to sleep the last night they spent together. Wil remarks, "That damn Tall," and shakes his head. Wil unfolds the poem and reads it to himself, then looks around the shop for an old picture frame. Finding a frame, Wil removes the back and places the poem in it, then replaces the back. Wil finds a nail and a hammer and heads to the house to place the poem on the wall. He looks all around the house and finally decides on a dimly lit spot halfway down the hall. As he is tacking the nail into the wall, Carla hears him and comes out of the room she is working in.

"What on earth are you doing, Wil?" Carla asks.

"Well, you asked me to clean out my duffel bag, didn't you?" Wil responds.

"Yes," Carla answers with a smile, "but I didn't know that meant pounding on the walls."

"Well, you know Tall," Wil begins. "He must have put this poem in my bag when I wasn't looking. I found it in there with a dime novel about Wyatt Earp. Tall read me this poem the last night we were together. It is one he wrote himself. He also told me I needed to grow a mustache like Wyatt Earp, so I'm sure that is why he put that in there. He had a bunch of those dime novels. Not sure what he did with the rest of them."

"Maybe you should give it a try, Wil," Carla says.

"Give what a try?" Wil queries.

"The mustache," Carla replies.

Wil just cocks his head and looks at Carla out of the corner of his eyes. Carla laughs. Wil turns and goes back to the shop. But Carla is curious about the poem and takes a moment to read it before returning to her room cleaning. As she is going back into the room, she turns her head to look back at the poem and says to herself, "A man thing, I think."

While Wil and Carla are adjusting their lives in preparation for the baby, Memory has been busy in New York. She has given birth to a son and has named him Jesse James, from one of the dime novels that Tall had given her. She has found a job in a factory in New York. She works long hours to earn enough money for her and Jesse. She doesn't like it, but while she is working, she must leave Jesse with an older woman who lives in the same apartment building. No matter how tired she is, after she picks Jesse up from the older woman, she feeds him supper and always reads to him from one of the dime novels after she tucks him in bed. She tells him about his wonderful father and how they must save enough money to go to Wyoming to a place there called the Hole in the Wall. There they will meet up with his father, and life will be wonderful.

Carla's time is getting near. She has been bedridden the last few days.

"Wil," Wil's mother beckons, "I think you better go get Jackie. Carla is getting close, and it's not going to be long now."

Without saying a word, Wil grabs his hat and heads out the door, gets in the old pickup, and heads for Jackie and Maxie's place. It is only a short distance, and Wil pulls into their driveway, jumps out of the truck, and begins calling to his grandmother, "Grandma, Grandma, Mom says you need to come now. Carla's time is here."

Maxie gets up from his chair and says, "You go on with Wil. Jackie and I'll be along in just a few minutes."

"Okay, Maxie," Jackie responds, taking off her apron, "just let me grab a few things."

Jackie gets in the truck with Wil, and they head back to the ranch house while Maxie, taking his time, gathers himself up, and follows along behind.

"When Maxie gets here, Wil," Jackie commands him, "the two of you go find something to do. This is women's work, and we won't need you two here in the way. We will call you when everything is finished."

Wil goes outside to wait for Maxie. Wil's mother is with Carla, and Jackie enters the bedroom to see how things are going. "How close are we?" Jackie asks.

"Pretty close now," Wil's mother responds.

"I'd better take a look," Jackie replies as she lifts the covers. "Yes, it won't be long now."

Wil and Maxie are in the shop. To Wil it seems like eternity. Maxie reaches into his pocket and pulls out a folding knife. Handing the knife to Wil, he says, "Here ya go, son. I made this for you a while back and wanted to wait until this day to give it to you."

"I don't know what to say, Gramps," Wil replies.

"Well," Maxie says with a breath, "thanks will be fine."

"Oh man," Wil states with embarrassment, "I don't know where my mind is right now. Thanks a bunch, Gramps."

The two laughs, and Maxie says, "Everything will be fine, son. Your grandmother has done this many times before. In fact, she brought you into this world a while back."

The two putters around the shop for a while. For Wil it seems like days have passed, and he finally breaks the silence. "Gramps, how long does this baby thing take? It seems like we have been here forever."

Maxie responds with a smile, "It takes as long as it takes, son. Seems to me I had the same conversation with your father when he was waiting on you to be born." With that, Maxie looks out the window and sees the shade on the kitchen window is now raised.

"Well," he says, grinning, "looks like the wait is over. Guess we better go find out if it's a boy or a girl."

Wil is out the shop door and entering the house before Maxie can get out of the shop. He swings the house door open and sees Jackie standing there. "Well?" he asks with enthusiasm.

"You have a fine son, Wil," Jackie replies. "Go on in and have a look, but you can't stay long. Carla is pretty tired right now."

Wil enters the room. Carla is lying in bed holding their son. Wil walks closer to get a good look at him. "It's a boy, Wil," Carla tells him.

"Yes, Jackie told me," Wil replies. "I couldn't be happier. How are you doing?"

"I'll be fine in a couple of days, once I've had some rest," Carla answers. "Here, Wil, hold your son."

Wil reaches down to pick up the baby but is very hesitant. "He's pretty little," Wil says. "I don't want to hurt him or anything." Carla smiles and hands him the newborn child. Wil cuddles him closely. Suddenly Wil looks over at Carla and says, "We haven't even discussed a name for him."

"No," Carla answers, "but I've been thinking about names for a long time. I would like to name him Shane. It means 'gift from God.'"

"Shane is a fine name," Wil replies, "and he certainly is a gift from God. Yes, Shane it is."

The years pass by quickly for both Shane Drury in Wyoming and Jesse James in New York City. While Shane spends much of his day helping his father and learning the ways of a cowboy, Jesse's days are spent with the other youth in the city, learning to navigate the back alleys in order to avoid the pursuit of the police. Shane is learning the love of the land and the ranching way of life, while Jesse is learning how to survive the tough city atmosphere. Yet in a short time, both families will experience lifechanging events that will cause their trails to meet.

CHAPTER 3

LIFE CHANGES

The years pass by quickly, and Shane is growing into a fine young cowboy. He stays close by his father's side, learning to ride, rope, doctor cattle, hunt, and fish. He loves the country way of life and adapts quickly to all that his father teaches him. His father and he have developed a close bond, and he enjoys spending as much time together as they can.

One day, Shane suddenly takes ill and cannot get out of bed. His mother recognizes the fact that he is not up yet and goes in his room to check on him. Carla quickly recognizes that Shane is ill and kneels beside his bed, "What is it, Shane?" Carla asks.

But Shane cannot answer. He only moans. Carla touches Shane's forehead and realizes that he has a high fever. She quickly pulls off his covers. He is sweating profusely. "I'll be right back, Shane," Carla says and quickly leaves his room.

Wil is sitting at the kitchen table having his morning coffee when Carla comes in. "What's going on?" Wil asks.

"Shane is sick. He has a very high fever," Carla responds. "I need to tend to him right away."

Wil rushes to Shane's room. He looks at Shane lying there, soaking wet from his own sweat. "What's going on, son?" Wil asks, but Shane cannot answer. Wil reaches out and puts his hand on Shane's forehead, then leaves the room. He returns to the kitchen, "I'll go for Doc Cunningham."

"Yes," Carla agrees, "but on the way, stop and see if Sandra can come over. Perhaps Robert can bring her so you can go on to find Doc Cunningham."

"Sure, Carla, sure," Wil replies as he grabs his coat and hat. "I'll be as quick as I can."

Carla watches as the pickup pulls out of the driveway and then continues getting towels, washcloths, water, and rubbing alcohol to cool Shane down from his fever. Carla tends to Shane, cooling him down with the water and alcohol. She waits patiently for Sandra to arrive, with expectations that she may have a way to make Shane more comfortable until Doc Cunningham can arrive.

Carla hears a vehicle pull into the driveway, and she rushes to the door. It is Robert and Sandra Amis. The pickup stops, and Sandra gets out. Rushing to Carla, she gives her a hug and asks, "Are you okay, Carla?"

Carla nods and says, "It's Shane. He's got a bad fever, and I'm not sure what to do for him. I hope Wil can find Doc Cunningham."

Robert rolls down the window of the pickup and says, "I'm gonna head back to get the chores done, and I'll be back to check on things."

Sandra, still holding on to Carla, waves her hand in agreement. "Let's take a look at Shane," Sandra whispers to Carla, and they walk into the house and into Shane's room.

Sandra looks at Shane and says, "He's got a bad fever all right. Looks like you've done about everything we can do until Wil gets back with Doc Cunningham."

In New York, nearly ten years have passed since Memory arrived in America. Working as much as she could and trying to raise Jesse, she still hasn't been able to save up the money that she needs for them to make the trip west to Wyoming. Her days were spent working while her nights were spent reading the dime novels to Jesse and telling him how someday, they would make the trip west to live with his father.

Jesse listens intently to the stories from the dime novels and is intrigued by the western outlaw way of life. While outside playing, he often pretends that he is one of the outlaws from the dime novels. He knows all the back alleys and pretends that one alley in particular is the Hole in the Wall, and occasionally he will go past a street vendor or enter a store, grab something, and take off running, eluding the police, who only halfheartedly pursue him.

Memory is beginning to get very ill. She forces herself to continue working, but as each day passes, she becomes weaker and weaker, unable to attend work on many occasions. This puts a strain on the household income, and she is unsure how she will be able to continue to support Jesse and herself. She does not know where she can turn for help.

She is aware that Jesse is bringing home food items, but he has no money to buy them. She can't help but think that if she doesn't do something very soon, Jesse will get into serious trouble.

Memory remembers that there was an orphanage that she would pass by on her way to work. Several times she has put the thought out of her mind, but now realizes that she must do something. So, one day while Jesse is out playing, she musters her strength and makes her way to the orphanage. She knocks on the door and is greeted by a priest.

"I must speak with you about my son," Memory replies. "Please, can I come in and talk with you?"

"Of course," the priest answers and beckons Memory inside. "Please have a seat. And what is it about your son that you must speak with me?" the priest inquires.

Memory begins to explain as she sits down, "I am not from this country, but came here some years ago after meeting an American soldier who helped rescue me when the Germans invaded my country. He told me of his ranch in Wyoming, and I have been trying to get there with my son. The child is his son also, but he doesn't know. Now I have become very ill, and I will probably never be able to make the trip west with my son, but I would very much like for him to have the opportunity for him to find his father."

"Well," the priest begins, "I am not sure how I can help you. We are an orphanage, and it is our goal to try to find homes for the orphans, not to give them passage to wherever."

Memory begins to cry. "You must help me, Father," she sobs. "I am afraid that if I cannot leave my son here, he will surely get into trouble and never have any kind of a future. Surely you can take him in and somehow find a way for him to get to his father. You are my only hope. Please, Father, I beg you."

The priest knows that he cannot fulfill Memory's request, but tells her, "I will take the boy in and care for him. I believe there is a way to get him passage to the west. We have a train that takes the orphans to western locations where they can be adopted into loving families. Perhaps your son can get on the train and get out west. We will certainly care for him as if he were one of our own."

Wiping her tears, Memory states, "Thank you, Father, and bless you. I will bring him by tomorrow. I don't know yet what I will tell him, but please you must not let him know that I am not well."

"Surely, he already knows that" the priest responds, "but I will say nothing of it if that is your wish. Bring the boy by tomorrow, and we will take him in."

Rising from her chair, Memory again says, "Thank you, Father, thank you."

As Memory leaves the orphanage, the priest beckons one of the sisters.

"Sister Margaret," the priest calls out.

"Yes, Father," Sister Margaret says, "what is it?"

"Tomorrow," the priest begins, "we have a boy coming in to the orphanage. He has been running rampant on the streets as his mother is too ill to care for him. I suspect he will be trouble, and I want to get him on a train as soon as possible."

Yes, Father," Sister Margaret replies, "I will find out when the next train leaves and see that he has passage."

"Very good," the priest states. "That is all."

That evening, Memory talks with Jesse, "Jesse, you know how much I love you and want only the best for you, don't you?"

"Why yes, Momma," Jesse agrees. "What is it? Why are you crying? Is it because you are ill?"

"Oh, Jesse," Memory begins, "you are such a smart boy. Your momma is going to be okay, but for now I need you to go ahead of me west to find your father, and I will come along later. I have been missing a lot of work, and I can no longer care for you the way I need to, so please, you must go on ahead of me."

"But I don't want to go without you, Momma," Jesse states.

"It is the only way, son," Memory states sternly as she reaches for Jesse's pack. "If there were anything else that I could do, I would certainly do it. Now listen to me. I have packed some things for you. Here in this pack are the dime novels that I have read to you. There is also your father's knife. You will be able to use it to help locate your father, his first name is on it. I have also given you this card. It is the queen of diamonds. You can pretend it is a picture of me. Always keep it with you, and it will keep you safe. I am afraid that is all I have to send with you. Just remember that I love you, and you will be just fine."

Jesse reluctantly agrees with a nod of his head.

"Tomorrow, we will go, and I will leave you with a nice man who is going to find a way for you to get out west," Memory tells Jesse. "So, sleep well tonight, my son, and we will get you on your way in the morning."

"Good night, Momma," Jesse says and heads off to bed. "I love you, Momma."

The next morning, Jesse, and Memory walk slowly to the orphanage. Arriving, Memory knocks on the door. Again, the priest answers the door, but when Jesse realizes where he is, he become upset. "Please, Momma," Jesse begs, "don't make me go in there, please. I want to go with you, Momma. Please let me go with you," Jesse begs over and over.

"No, son," Memory says to Jesse, "you cannot go with me. You must stay here. I love you more than anything in this world, Jesse, but you cannot go with me."

With tears filling her eyes, Memory gives Jesse's hand to the priest, who takes him inside. Memory turns and walks away, but she is sad and very weak. She only makes it around the corner from the orphanage, and she collapses.

Wil arrives back at the ranch with Doc Cunningham.

"Where is the boy?" Doc Cunningham asks Carla. "I'd better get a look at him."

Carla motions for Doc Cunningham to go with her to Shane's room. "He's pretty sick, Wendell," Carla whispers, and they enter Shane's room.

Doc Cunningham looks Shane over very closely. "He's got the fever, all right," Doc Cunningham states, "but it looks like there is more than that going on. The fever should have let up with the water and alcohol bath. The next twenty-four hours should tell us what is going on. I'll give him something to help him rest. I'm afraid he's going to need his strength."

Wil has come into the room. "He's a strong boy, Doc," Wil states. "He will pull through this. He has to."

Wil goes over to Shane and places his hand on his forehead. Shane's eyes open, and he looks up at his father. "I'm sorry, Dad," Shane says in a very weak voice.

"Sorry for what, son?" Wil responds. "Everyone gets a little sick now and then. You're gonna be just fine."

"Let him rest for now," Doc Cunningham tells Wil and Carla. "I'll stay the night and keep a watch on him. You guys had better get some rest yourselves."

Wil and Carla leave the room while Doc Cunningham settles into a chair next to Shane.

Wil is awake all night, worrying about Shane. He gets up very early in the morning to check on Shane. "Any change, Doc?" Wil asks.

"I'm afraid I have bad news, Wil," Doc Cunningham replies. "You had better get Carla."

"What is it, Doc?" Wil insists.

"Shane has slipped into a coma, Wil," Doc Cunningham answers. "There is just nothing more than I can do for him."

"There must be something, Doc," Wil states.

Doc Cunningham simply says, "No, I'm sorry, Wil."

Wil reluctantly goes for Carla. They enter Shane's room together. "I'll give you some time to spend with him alone," Doc Cunningham tells them as he leaves the room.

Only a short time passes, and Shane takes his last breath. Carla begins to cry and lays her head on Shane's chest. Wil touches her back and without saying a word, walks out of the room.

CHAPTER 4

HEADING WEST

Jesse is at the orphanage a very short time before he is put on the orphan train and heading west to some unknown destination. It is fine with Jesse, as he did not like being at the orphanage. He is excited about heading west but knows he must figure out how to get to Wyoming. He has been told that he will be adopted by a family somewhere in the Midwest, an idea that he is not in favor of. All he needs to do is get to Wyoming and then he can find his father. As the train is traveling across Nebraska, an announcement is made that the train will be stopping in Cheyenne, Wyoming, to refuel. No one is to leave the train at Cheyenne as they will be traveling south from there to one of the adoption destinations. They will have lunch on the train while it is refueling. Jesse knows that this will be his chance and must figure out a way to sneak off the train.

The whistle blows, and the train pulls slowly up to the Cheyenne station. Jesse, holding his pack very tightly, anxiously awaits his opportunity to escape. With any luck, he can slip quietly off the train unnoticed. From that point on, even if it were discovered that he was no longer on the train, no one would care.

The other orphans are gawking out the windows of the train, and the chaperones are busy getting lunch ready for the children. With all the distractions, Jesse makes his way quietly to the rear of the car, carefully opening the rear door just wide enough to squeeze out. He throws his pack out first and then slips through the opening, quietly closing the door behind him. One of the chaperones looks up and around the train. Seeing nothing out of the ordinary, she goes back to working with the other chaperones preparing lunches for the orphans.

Jesse is now free from the train but must hurry to distance himself so that no one will recognize him as one of the orphans. He quickly finds a store and slips in, hoping to hide out until the train leaves. Fortunately, all the orphans were given newer clothes to wear on the trip to their adoption, and Jesse does not look the part of an orphan. There are other people in the store, and Jesse just wanders around, hoping that he can mingle in unnoticed. It seems like an eternity while Jesse is waiting to hear the train leave the station, but the time comes, and he breathes a sigh of relief, thinking that his escape has been successful, and with that thought in mind, he leaves the store. Now he must get out of Cheyenne before someone notices that he has escaped from the train.

Jesse remembers that he saw some cattle trucks at the stockyards as the train pulled into Cheyenne. No matter where they are going, if he can sneak a ride, they will get him out of Cheyenne. So, with pack in tow, he makes his way to the stockyards and finds the drivers deep in jovial conversation. They are not paying any attention to their trucks, so Jesse very carefully sneaks into the cab of one of the trucks and hides in the rear compartment. He listens carefully to the drivers as they discuss their next destination. He hears one of the drivers say that he is headed north to pick up another load of cattle and bring them back to Cheyenne. Jesse looks content, as no matter where this truck takes him, he will escape Cheyenne, and when the time is right, he will get out of the truck and begin his search for his father.

As the driver is heading north in his truck just past Casper, he gets a feeling that there is something strange with his truck. He is not sure what it is but decides that maybe he had better pull over and look things over. While the truck is parked along the side of the road, Jesse plans his escape from the truck. He looks in the mirror at the trucker as he is walking around his truck and trailer. When the trucker goes to the far side of his trailer, Jesse quietly slips out of the truck and hides along the side of the road in the sagebrush until the trucker pulls away.

Once the truck has left, Jesse comes out of hiding. At this point, he is not sure where he should go, so he continues to walk north to the next town, where he will start his search. Unfortunately for Jesse, his clever luck is about to run out. Sheriff Richards, from Kaycee, is heading to Casper but notices Jesse walking along the road. He thinks out loud, mumbling, "That is pretty strange for a young boy to be hiking this far out of Casper all by himself. I had better swing around and check this out." With that being said, Sheriff Richards finds a spot where he can turn his squad car back north and pulls up behind Jesse.

At this point, Jesse decides it would be futile to try to run, but he whispers under his breath, "Damn."

Jesse stops and sets his backpack down. Sheriff Richards turns on his lights and stops behind Jesse.

"Where you headed, son?" Sheriff Richards asks as he gets out of his car. But Jesse does not answer. "Okay," Sheriff Richards says, "how about, where are you from then?"

Jesse is just standing there, looking down at his backpack. "Well," Sheriff Richards begins, "maybe you had better come with me until we can get all this figured out. You are pretty young to be out here on your own. You must belong to someone, and that means you are either running away from something or running to something. You know, boy, I just might be able to help you, but you are gonna have to talk to me."

Sheriff Richards reaches down for Jesse's pack, but Jesse grabs it and holds it close to his chest. "Okay, boy," Sheriff Richards responds, "you hold on to it, but you are gonna have to get in the car, and sooner or later I'm gonna have to see what's in there. We're okay for now, though." With that, Sheriff Richards escorts Jesse to the back of the squad car and closes the door.

Jesse is very forlorn at this point. He was so close, and now he is captive with no way to escape. He will have to tell the sheriff his story, and just perhaps, he will help.

It is a silent ride back to Kaycee, although Sheriff Richards tries to get Jesse to talk.

"So, you want to tell me anything about yourself, son? You know, I just might be able to help you. You are either running away from something or going to something. I really can't help you if you won't tell me anything. I really am a pretty nice person. I have a couple of boys that are right around your age. Maybe you would like to meet them. You know the first thing I have to figure out is where I am going to put you. My wife's name is Judy. Me and Judy have been together quite a few years now. She would want me to bring you home, but there really isn't any room for any more people in that little house that we have. I sure wish you would let me help you. If you don't, I will probably have to send you to the orphanage in Cheyenne. My guess is that may be where you came from." Sheriff Richards looks back at Jesse in the rearview mirror several times while he is talking to him, but Jesse never shows any expression until Sheriff Richards mentions the orphanage. At that point, he looks up at Sheriff Richards and makes eye contact in the mirror. "Well, looks like I said something that got your attention. So, you are from the orphanage." By this time, they are pulling into the Kaycee sheriff's station. "Well, this is as far as we go for now, son. You will have to come inside with me until we hash this all out." Sheriff Richards says as he gets out of the car and opens Jesse's door, "You'll have to come along with me now, son. Won't you at least tell me your name so I can stop calling you son?"

"Jesse," Jesse states firmly. "My name is Jesse James!"

"Well." Sheriff Richards chuckles as he escorts Jesse inside the Sheriff station. "Now we're getting somewhere."

Once they are inside, Sheriff Richards says, "Well, Jesse James, I guess I'm going to have to put you in a cell for the time being."

Jesse stops and asks, "Well, Sheriff, maybe we can make a deal. If you don't lock me up, I won't try to run away. What do you think? They locked me up at the orphanage, and I didn't like being locked up."

"So," Sheriff Richards starts, "you were in the orphanage in Cheyenne then."

"No, Sheriff," Jesse responds, "I was in an orphanage, but not in Cheyenne."

"Where then?" Sheriff Richards queries.

"In New York City," Jesse answers.

"New York City!" Sheriff Richards repeats, shocked. "How the heck did you get from New York City to Wyoming, pray tell?"

"I was put on a train with other orphans to be adopted by families in the west," Jesse begins, "but I wanted to find my family that is here in Wyoming and not go to some family that I am not kin to."

"We are getting somewhere now, Jesse," Sheriff Richards states. "I'll tell you what, Jesse, why don't you call me Dale instead of Sheriff? It will be okay. We will be friends, and I will do everything I can to help you find your family. So, what information do you have that can help us locate your family? Can you just start out from the beginning and give me the whole story?"

"You promise that I can trust you?" Jesse asks.

"You sure don't trust people very easily, do you, Jesse?" Sheriff Richards answers back. "Yes, I promise you can trust me, and I will help you, but I need as much information as you can give me. Start out with how you got in the New York City orphanage in the first place."

And so, Jesse begins with his story, "So, Dale, I was born in New York City. My mother came here from Europe with the hope of coming west to find my father. She did not know much about him."

"And what was your mother's name?" Sheriff Richards interrupts.

"Her name is Memory," Jesse continues. "She met my father during the war. He helped to evacuate our city. He does not know about me. My mother told me everything, well, almost. She didn't tell me she was ill, but I knew. She said I should go on ahead, and she would come along later, but I know that will never happen. She gave me these things and told me they would help me find my father."

Jesse picks up his pack and opens it.

"Do you know your father's name?" Sheriff Richards asks.

Reaching into the pack, Jesse continues, "Well, not exactly. But I have his knife here. He carried it during the war and gave it to my mother. It has a name on it. It says, 'Wil.'" Jesse takes the knife out of the pack and hands it to Sheriff Richards.

Sheriff Richards reaches out for the knife. "That is a beautiful knife, Jesse. It looks like it was handmade. But we will need a lot more to go on than a knife. What else do you have in there?"

"Not much," Jesse responds. "I have these books that belonged to my father and a card that my mother gave to me. She said it should remind me of her. It is the queen of diamonds." Jesse hands the books and the card to the sheriff. "She said I should always keep the card with me, and it will keep me safe, just the same as if she were with me."

"This isn't much to go on," the sheriff states. "Do you know anything else?"

Jesse answers the sheriff, "She said I should go to Wyoming, to a place called the Hole in the Wall. Do you know of such a place?"

The Hole in the Wall?" Sheriff Richards questions. "Are you sure you didn't just get that out of one of these dime novels? Here, look at this one, Butch Cassidy and the Sundance Kid." Sheriff Richards holds up the book. "Butch Cassidy was the leader of the Hole in the Wall gang, and I'll bet it says so right in here."

"Yes," Jesse answers, "it does. My mother used to read the books to me all the time, and when she did, she would always say, 'That is where your father's ranch is.'"

"Okay," Sheriff Richards begins, "I have got to go and run some errands. Now remember, you promised that you would not run away."

Jesse nods his head, affirming that he did indeed promise.

Sheriff Richards continues, "Well, I'll tell you this right now. A promise made is a debt unpaid. Once you promise something, you owe that debt to the person you made the promise to, and the only way you can pay that debt is to keep that promise. Do you understand? I mean to hold you to your promise. I will keep my promise to you, but you also need to keep your promise to me. Are we okay?"

"Yes," Jesse replies, "I understand, and I will keep my promise to you. I hope you will do the same and help me find my father."

"I told you I would, and I will. You can bet on that," Sheriff Richards responds.

Sheriff Richards takes his hat from the hook on the wall and starts out the door, telling Jesse, "I'll be back soon, and I'll bring some supper for you. You must be getting hungry. Never seen a boy that wasn't hungry." Then Sheriff Richards goes out the door and gets into his squad car.

The squad car pulls up in front of the Kaycee country store. Sheriff Richards steps out of the car and makes his way inside. Seated at a little table are Roger Cappi and Darrell Snow, while Joanne Snow is busy behind the counter.

"Hey, everyone," Sheriff Richards says as he walks in. "Hello, Dale," Roger responds.

"Can I get you a cup of coffee, Sheriff?" Darrell asks.

"No, thanks," Dale replies, "I've had plenty of coffee today."

"What's eatin' you, Dale?" Roger asks. "You look like you got something on your mind."

"Well, I do have a bit of a dilemma on my hands," Dale begins as he now has the attention of all three of the people in the store. "I picked up this young boy walking along the road from Casper this morning. I hate to keep him at the jail, but me and Judy just don't have any room for him. I promised him I would not turn him over to the orphanage, and so that makes another problem."

"Why would you promise him something like that?" Joanne asks as she makes her way over to join the others.

"You know," Dale starts up again, "that is an interesting question, but it was the only way I could get him to talk, and once he started telling me his story, well, I just couldn't believe it. He's got a pretty wild imagination to come up with a story like that. It's quite a story, and I'm sure most of it comes from the dime novels he's got."

"Well, Dale," Roger demands, "don't keep us in the dark. Lay it out for us."

Dale explains, "He had this pack when I picked him up, and he was pretty attached to it. He wouldn't let me see what he had right off, but after I got him talking, he showed me what he had in there, and it kinda is stuff that backs up his story. I suspected he had run off from the orphanage in Cheyenne, but he claims he is from New York City, and got off the orphan train in Cheyenne. That's how I came to make the promise. He agreed to tell me his story if I promised not to lock him in a cell or take him to the orphanage."

"Okay," Darrell says, "but what was in the pack?"

"Hold on now," Dale quips, "you're getting ahead of the story. So, he says he is from New York City and has come to Wyoming to look for his father. For some reason, he thinks his father has a ranch somewhere near the Hole in the Wall. Now I didn't tell him that just by luck, the Hole is just west of here, and he really has no idea where it is other than it is in Wyoming, and that he could have gotten out of the dime novels he has with him. He even claims that his name is Jesse James. I just don't know about all this."

"Dime novels?" Roger questions.

"Yes," Dale answers, "dime novels, maybe a half dozen or so. Then he tells me that his mother was sick and couldn't care for him, which is how he got on the orphan train. Says she gave him an old playing card, the queen of diamonds, to keep him safe on his journey. But it gets better. He tells me this story of how his father helped to evacuate the village his mother lived in during WWI. He has this knife that he claims his father gave to his mother and told her it would help her find his ranch. He claims that his father didn't know about him because he was born in New York City after the war was over."

Roger asks, "So how could the knife help find the ranch? Was there anything special about it?"

"Now again," Dale says, "you're getting ahead of the story. It is a special knife, custom made, I believe. It has an insignia on it and the name 'Wil,' but other than that, I can't see how it helps."

"Well now, Dale," Roger says, reaching into his pocket. "That kid's story may not be so far-fetched after all." Pulling his own knife out of his pocket and handing it to Dale, Roger asks, "Did the knife look like this? It's a Mehaffey. Maxie made it for me years ago. He didn't make very many of them."

Dale looks the knife over and states, "That is exactly the insignia that is on his knife, and his has the name Wil on it."

"Dale," Roger replies. "You haven't been around these parts as long as some of us. Maxie and Jackie Mehaffey were Tall and Wil Drury's grandparents. Maxie made a knife for each of them when they went off to war. They were both over there in Europe somewhere, and their ranch is part of the Hole in the Wall. Tall never made it back from the war, and Wil would never talk about it. You know, my sister Carla is married to Wil. I'd better go and have a chat with them. Looks like Wil might be this kid's father. That ain't gonna go over too good."

"Go over too good?" Dale questions. "Why, that ain't gonna go over at all, and I would be the last one that would want to confront Wil Drury about this. Why, he ain't been sober one day since that boy died, and he's gotten real mean. You just might be walkin' into a big fight. I'm not sure how this should be handled."

"Why don't you just let me talk to Wil and Carla and see what happens?" Roger inquires. "And I ain't so dumb as to go talk to Wil on my own. I'm gonna stop by and get Robert Amis. Robert has been really good to Wil, especially since Shane died. He would never pick a fight with Robert."

"Well," Dale begins, "I told, that boy I would help him if I could. Just maybe I've come to the right people. Just remember, Roger, I don't want any trouble out there."

Roger puts on his hat, picks his walking stick out of the corner, and heads out the door. "Thanks for the coffee, Joanne. I'll be seeing you, Darrell. Have a good day, Dale, and I'll let you know how things go out at the ranch," Roger says as he leaves.

CHAPTER 5

RIDDLE SOLVED

The dust blows up as Roger takes off in his pickup, headed for the ranch where Wil and his sister Carla live. His pickup pulls into the Amis residence, and he sees Robert and Sandra sitting on the front porch. Robert gets up to meet Roger as his pickup comes to a stop in front of the house.

"Howdy," Roger yells out. "How is everyone here?"

"We're doing just fine," Robert replies. "Why don't you sit and have a glass of sweet tea with Sandra and me? We can visit a spell."

"That would be just great," Roger responds, "but I'm afraid I've come to ask you to accompany me over to Wil and Carla's."

"Is there something wrong?" Robert asks.

"It's kind of a long story and a bit complicated," Roger tells Robert. "I can explain on the way."

Robert turns to Sandra and says, "I need to go with Roger."

Sandra interrupts, "I heard. You can tell me all about it when you get back. You men just go on and do what you need to do."

So, Roger and Robert load into Roger's truck and head toward the Drury ranch. Roger explains everything to Robert as best he can and is just finishing up when they pull into Wil's driveway. Roger finishes up, "And so, I've got to explain everything I know to Wil and Carla to see what they want to do. This whole thing could blow up with Wil being so mean these days."

"You know," Robert begins, "I'll bet there is a lot more to this thing than we know. Maybe Wil will take it all in stride and help us find out the facts. That war was quite a while ago."

The two men get out of the truck and are met by Carla, who asks, "Well, how nice of you to come visit. To what do I owe this?"

"Carla," Roger states, "I kinda need to talk with you and Wil. Is Wil around?"

"I'm sure he's around here somewhere," Carla replies. "I imagine he's out checking the livestock. What is all this about?"

"I'd kinda like to talk to both of you at the same time," Roger says. "It has to do with Wil's war days, and well, it's gonna take some explaining."

Robert has already gone to look for Wil and finds him just as he is returning from the pasture. Robert waves to Wil and asks, "How's it going, neighbor?"

Wil grumbles, "Ain't nothing changes around here except people dying."

"I know losing that boy was tough on you, Wil," Robert answers, "but there ain't no sense killing yourself over it. Things like that just happen."

"They don't just happen," Wil replies. "So, to what do I owe this visit?"

"I came out here with Roger," Robert tells Wil. "He's in the house and needs to talk to you and Carla."

"About what?" Wil demands.

"Come on to the house and we'll see," Robert answers.

Wil reaches into the feed bin and pulls out a bottle of whisky, takes a sip, puts it back, and says, "Well, let's get this over with. I doubt it will amount to much if it's something Roger has to talk about." And with that, the two men walk to the house.

Roger tells Carla and Wil everything that Sheriff Richards told him about the boy and the items he has in his pack. They listen carefully but say not a word until finally Wil has heard enough.

"Now let me get this straight, Roger," Wil stands up and says, "Sheriff Richards picks up some runaway. He's got dime novels and a knife, and you think he was coming here. Now have I got that right so far?"

"Now, Wil, I'm just repeating what Dale told me," Roger exclaims. "He said the boy had a pretty good story, and I didn't think much about it until he said the knife was custom made. I showed him my knife, you know, the one Maxie made for me, and Dale said the boy's knife has the same insignia. Not only that but it has your name on it."

Wil's mind flashes back to the night when he and Tall exchanged knives. "I want to see the boy," Wil states firmly.

"What are you thinking, Wil?" Carla asks.

Reaching for his hat, Wil replies, "Come on, we're going to town. There are some things I have to know."

Roger and Robert load up in Roger's pickup while Wil and Carla get into theirs. Wil and Carla head into town, and Roger takes Robert back home.

Wil and Carla arrive at the sheriff's station and go inside. "Hello, Sheriff," Wil states. "I heard there is a boy here with some rather strange stories of how he got here."

"That's a good way to put it," Sheriff Richards replies. "Roger Cappi must have talked to you. He said he was going out to your place to talk to you. I'm glad you came in to see the boy so we can talk about his story."

"Where is he?" Wil questions.

"He just went outside for a minute. He'll be back," Sheriff Richards answers. "Why don't you and Carla have a seat?"

"Can I see his things?" Wil asks.

"I better wait 'til he comes back in," Sheriff Richards replies. "He's pretty touchy about them. They are the only thing he has in the world. Now Roger tells me that you were in WWI, over in Europe somewhere."

"That's right," Wil states firmly. "I was in that damn war with my brother, Tall. Tall didn't make it back." Wil has a flashback of his last radio contact with his brother Tall.

"I'm sorry to hear that," Sheriff Richards tells Wil. "Here comes the boy now," Sheriff Richards states as Jesse comes through the door.

Jesse is wearing one of Sheriff Richards's cowboys hats and has a big smile on his face as he walks into the room. Wil takes one look at him and has a flashback to when Tall was about the same age as Jesse and sees that he looks exactly like Tall.

"Jesse," Sheriff Richards begins, "this is Wil and Carla Drury, and I would like for you to tell them your story and show them the things you have in your pack."

Jesse has learned to trust Sheriff Richards and begins by getting his pack. "Well," Jesse starts, "I don't have much, and I am here trying to find my father's ranch. He said it was by the Hole in the Wall, and my mother gave me some things that he gave her so that I could show them to him, and he would know who I am."

"Now, son," Wil says.

"My name is Jesse," Jesse states, "Jesse James."

"Very well, Jesse," Wil says in agreement. "So how do you know about the Hole in the Wall? You are too young to have heard that from your father."

"Do you know my father?" Jesse asks Wil.

"I'm not sure, maybe," Wil replies. "I need to see what you have there and ask you some questions before we know for sure."

"Okay," Jesse answers, "my mother explained everything to me that I know. She used to read these dime novels to me and tell me all about my father."

Jesse reaches into his pack and gets out the dime novels. They are old and worn, and as he hands them to Wil, Wil's mind flashes back to Tall buying the dime novels.

"Yes," Wil says, "and what else do you have?"

"I got this knife," Jesse says, "that my mother said my father gave to her. It is a special knife and has a name on it. Actually, the name on it is Wil. Isn't that your name?"

"Yes," Wil replies, "let's have a look at that knife."

Jesse gets the knife out of his pack and hands it to Wil. Wil opens the knife and sees immediately that it is his knife. Wil has a flashback to the night that he and Tall exchanged knives.

"What is your mother's name?" Wil asks while looking at the knife.

"Memory," Jesse answers immediately.

"Memory," Wil repeats as his mind flashes back to Tall saying, "Let's just say I'll have a fond *memory* of this one."

"Memory," Wil mumbles again. "Well, I'll be damned."

"Did you know her?" Carla turns to Wil and asks.

"No," Wil answers firmly.

Jesse reaches into his pack and pulls out the queen of diamonds playing card and hands it to Wil. "My mother gave me this," Jesse says. "She said it came from a soldier, and it would keep me safe as long as I always carried it with me."

"I can't believe it," Wil responds as his mind wanders off to a flashback of throwing the card to the woman in the crowd. "Carla, I saw her. It was in New York City as we were being bussed through the crowded streets. I knew immediately that there was something special about her but couldn't put it together at the time. This is one of the cards I threw from the bus. I'm sure of it."

"So," Carla says sadly, "you did know her then."

"No," Wil replies sternly, "I said I saw her."

"Sir," Jesse asks, "are you, my father?"

Both Sheriff Richards and Carla look at Wil, waiting for him to answer.

"No, Jesse," Wil answers as he sees Carla release a deep breath, "but I know who your father is."

Jesse's eyes light up as he asks, "Can you take me to him?"

"I'm afraid there are some things you need to know, Jesse," Wil responds.

"Maybe you could fill us all in," Sheriff Richards says as Carla nods in agreement.

"There is no easy way to tell you this, Jesse," Wil begins. "Your father never came back from the war."

"What are you saying?" Carla interrupts.

"I'm getting to that," Wil responds sharply. "You see, the night before we evacuated the town, Tall and I exchanged knives so that we could have a memento just in case one of us didn't make it. I have Tall's knife at the ranch. I asked Tall what I should do with his knife if he didn't make it out of there, and you know Tall, always talking in riddles. Well, he said to give it to his firstborn. He told me he had been seeing a girl in the town. When I asked her name, all he would say is that he would have a fond memory of her. You see, we now know her name was Memory."

"So, you are saying that Jesse is Tall's son?" Carla asks.

"It sure looks that way," Wil answers. "Those are the dime novels that Tall bought all but the one I have. He gave me the one of Wyatt Earp so I would grow a mustache like Earp had. He kept the rest, and I never knew what happened to them. They weren't with his things. He must have gone into town after I went to sleep and given them and my knife to Memory. I knew when I was throwing the cards out the bus window and saw that woman that there was something special about her, but how could I have known?"

Jesse is saddened to hear the news of his father and a bit afraid of what will happen to him now.

"What about your mother?" Wil asks Jesse.

Looking down at the floor, Jesse replies, "I don't know for sure, but she was sick when I left New York. She tried to hide it from me, but I knew. Otherwise, she would have never put me in that orphanage."

"I'm sorry, Jesse," Wil says solemnly. "We'd better go now, Carla."

Both Wil and Carla stand up to leave. As Sheriff Richards stands up, he says, "I'll walk you out."

"What will happen to the boy now, Sheriff?" Carla asks as she is getting into the pickup.

"Please, call me Dale," Sheriff Richards tells Carla. "As far as the boy goes, it's going to depend on you and Wil. You are the only kin the boy has left. I will send a wire to try to find his mother, but I doubt that will be very successful."

"Thanks, Dale," Carla says with a sigh. "I guess Wil and I have some things to talk about."

Wil and Carla headed back to the ranch. Not a word is said until the truck pulls into the driveway. Carla looks over at Wil as the pickup comes to a stop in front of the house.

"What are you thinking, Wil?" Carla asks.

Wil looks over at Carla and says, "I think I need to have a talk with Tall and Shane."

Carla gets out of the truck and walks into the house without saying another word. While Will heads to the barn. In the barn, Wil gets his bottle of whisky out of the feed bin and heads to the little graveyard to talk to Tall and Shane.

Standing by the little wooden fence of the graveyard, Wil begins to talk to Tall. "Well, brother, I guess the riddle is solved." Wil takes a sip of whisky and continues, "So I guess you were right. You have a firstborn after all. I guess that means I need to give him your knife. Remember when you told me that? You didn't know, did you? He's a fine young man and looks exactly like you when you were his age. Shane, little buddy, I think you know what I've got on my mind. There is no one that could ever replace you in my heart, but this boy is kin, and it just wouldn't be right to not take him in. He's tough like you were, so I hope you don't mind. I know without your mother saying anything that she would want to take Tall's son in and raise him as our own. Your uncle Tall would have taken you in if something had happened to me. That's just how we do things here." Wil takes another sip of whisky. "I'll go back and tell Carla that we have to take him in." Wil heads back to the barn to put the whisky back in the feed bin and then goes to the house.

Carla is sitting in the living room with her bible as Wil walks in and says, "I guess we had better tell Sheriff Richards that we will take the boy in and care for him. He's got no one else, and it's what Tall would want. I don't think Shane would mind."

"You really mean it, Wil?" Carla asks.

"It's the right thing to do," Wil replies.

CHAPTER 6

♠ ♣ ♥ ♦

RANCH LIFE

Jesse is taken in by Wil and Carla to begin life as their son. He is eager to learn things about ranching and being a cowboy.

"Uncle Wil," Jesse begins, "will you teach me how to rodeo?"

"Well, sure, son," Wil replies, "I'll teach you all about cowboying. You might even be as good a cowboy as your father."

"And shooting, Uncle Wil," Jesse asks with wide open eyes, "will you teach me to shoot?"

"One thing at a time now, son," Wil responds. "So where should we start?"

"I sure would like to learn to ride bulls," Jesse states.

"Ride bulls?" Wil asks. "You sure are in a hurry to get yourself stomped on. Maybe we should start out by putting you on one of the yearlings and let you work your way up to bulls. Let's see if we can run one in and see how you do on your first try."

"Sure, Uncle Wil," Jesse says with excitement, "let's run one in and I'll get on him."

Wil gets a rope, and he and Jesse run a couple yearlings into the chutes. "You want to ride with your left hand or right hand?" Wil asks Jesse.

"I'm not sure, Uncle Wil," Jesse replies. "Maybe we'll have to try each one out to see what works best for me."

"Okay, Jesse," Wil says as Jesse is getting on the yearling, "let's give it a try."

Jesse settles down on the yearling, and Wil opens the gate, but it's a short ride, and Jesse is bucked off. Instead of getting up and running to the fence, Jesse just lies on the arena floor. Wil runs over to him, takes him by the hand, and says, "Don't just lay there, son. You gotta get up and head to the fence. Why, if that were a real bull, he'd be doing a tap dance all over you. Let's try it again."

"He kinda knocked the wind out of me," Jesse says sheepishly. "I'll be more ready this next time."

Before long, Jesse approaches Wil and asks, "Can you teach me how to shoot now, Uncle Wil? I'd sure like to start hunting and bagging game rather than just tagging along with you."

"I guess you're old enough to learn to shoot," Wil tells Jesse. "Let me get us something to shoot with, and we'll go out to the prairie dog town."

Wil goes to the house, brings out a rifle, and he and Jesse head out into the pasture. Once they arrive at the prairie dog town, Wil tells Jesse, "Now the first thing we have to do is see which eye is your shooting eye."

"How do we do that?" Jesse asks.

"It's pretty simple," Wil responds. "Here now, hold up one finger, and with both eyes open, look at a fence post. Then close one eye and then open it and close the other eye. One eye will keep your finger on the fence post, and the other will move it off. The one that keeps your eye on the post is your shooting eye."

"That sounds simple enough," Jesse tells Wil and holds out his finger. "I guess I must have a left shooting eye, 'cause that's the one that stays on the post. My right eye moves it off."

"Well," Wil says with a grin, "I'm not surprised. Your father was a left-handed shooter. The only problem with that is all the bolt action rifles are made for right-handers. You'll just have to learn how to make that work for you just like Tall did. You're pretty good at everything else, so I don't guess you'll have any problem with that."

Just like the bull riding, Jesse excels quickly in the art of shooting.

Now Jesse is in his mid-teens and has mastered his rodeo skills to the point that some of the other teenagers in the area don't like to compete against him. Some of them get together and try to pick fights with Jesse, but Jesse is big and tough and can always hold his own. His room is decorated with buckles from the various rodeos that he has won and several shooting trophies. He is a tough competitor and doesn't like to lose at anything.

One summer day, Jesse accompanies Wil and Carla on a short trip to Casper. Jesse has a few dollars in his pocket and decides to wander off on his own while Wil and Carla attend to their business. As Jesse is going past a tattoo parlor, he notices something in the window that catches his eye. It is a design for aces and eights. Jesse recalls the significance of the aces and eights from the dime novel he read about Wild Bill Hickok and decides that he is going to get it tattooed on his chest just to show the other boys that he is tough beyond words.

Jesse meets up with Wil and Carla. They are finished with their business in Casper and jump in the pickup to head back home to the ranch.

"What did you do today in town, Jesse?" Carla asks.

"Well," Jesse responds, "I got this really great tattoo."

"You did what?" Carla snaps.

"I got a tattoo," Jesse says again as he opens his shirt to show her. "Two black aces and two black eights, the hand of cards Wild Bill was holding when he was shot."

"What on earth made you do something like that?" Carla inquires.

"I just want to show the other guys that if they are going to start something with me that I am going to see it through to the end," Jesse explains.

"You mean you have been having some trouble with some of the other guys?" Wil demands.

"Nothing I can't handle, Uncle Wil," Jesse states. "Just seems like they don't think it's right for me to do so well at the rodeos, and so they try to start fights with me. I guess they think it will get me kicked out of the competition or something."

"I don't like to hear that," Wil tells Jesse. "I don't want you getting into any kind of trouble, and I know how easily that kind of stuff can lead to trouble."

Carla looks over at Wil and says, "Seems you and Tall got into a few scuffles during the rodeos yourselves, especially when you two would take first and second place."

"That's exactly why I am saying that I know this kind of stuff can lead to big trouble," Wil states in his defense.

"Ah," Jesse says, "it ain't nothin' I can't handle, Uncle Wil. No need to worry. They'll never get the best of me."

"And that's just what I'm worried about," Wil tells Jesse.

It is a quiet ride home the rest of the way to the ranch.

As the years go by, just as Wil had feared, Jesse begins to get into trouble. It is just small skirmishes at first; however, each time they become a little more serious. Jesse is at a rodeo, and as usual he has won some money. As he is standing in line at the pay window, two flies land on his arm. With a swift scoop, he attempts to catch both flies, but only manages to capture one. As the other flies away, the cowboy behind him begins to laugh and says, "Ha, you missed."

"Oh, you think so?" Jesse challenges. "I'll tell you what I'll do. I'll bet my pay money against yours that I have a fly right here in my hand."

The cowboy responds, "I know you don't. I saw it fly away. Not sure why you want to waste your money, but I'll take that bet."

Jesse crushes the fly in his hand and then opens it.

"There ain't no way," the cowboy states with doubt. "I saw it fly away. This is some kind of trick or something."

"A bet is a bet," Jesse demands, "I'll be right beside you when you pick up your money."

"Well," the cowboy starts, "I ain't payin' you. I need that money to get me down the road. Besides, you tricked me."

Jesse gets his money, folds it up, puts it in his pocket, and patiently waits beside the cowboy while he gets his money.

"Pay up," Jesse tells the cowboy.

"I told you I ain't gonna pay," the cowboy replies as he puts his money in his pocket.

"Then I guess I'll just have to take it out of your hide," Jesse answers and begins by placing a left fist directly to the side of the cowboy's jaw. The cowboy drops to the ground, and Jesse gives him a good kick to the ribs and says, "Get up and take your lickin'."

The cowboy gets up slowly, and just as he is erect, Jesse lands another punch and then stomps the cowboy on the ground.

Sheriff Richards sees the fight, runs over, and grabs Jesse from behind. "What is this all about, Jesse?" the sheriff asks.

"He crawfished on a bet, so I took what he owed me out of his hide," Jesse tells the sheriff.

"Jesse," Sheriff Richards explains, "I have warned you in the past that fighting is not how we handle things. Besides, regardless of what the bet was about, I am not going to allow you to be beating up on people. I want you to go and leave this guy alone. The next time I have to intervene, I will put you in jail. You understand?"

Jesse just mumbles and walks away.

Hardly a week goes by, and Jesse is in town again. This time it is in the evening, and Jesse stops in Ron Vegh's saloon for a beer. There is only one stool available, so Jesse takes a seat and orders a beer. In the mirror, he notices a woman walk in the bar. She walks up behind the men seated on the barstools, walks to the left and then to the right, eventually stopping directly behind Jesse.

"Aren't any of you gentlemen going to offer a lady a place to sit?" the woman queries.

"Well," Jesse says as he turns around and removes his cowboy hat. Then with his hand, he brushes off his face and says, "Let me dust you off a place."

The men on each side of Jesse grab him by the arms, take him to the door, and throw him into the street. Jesse is infuriated by this and goes back into the bar.

"I don't want any trouble in here, Jesse," the owner and bartender, Ron Vegh, says to Jesse.

"Now that is going to depend on whether or not these two chickenshit bastards come outside or not," Jesse replies.

The two men do not even turn around, so Jesse kicks the barstool out from under one of them and throws the other to the floor. The fight begins, and Jesse is holding his own against the two, first knocking one to the floor and then the other. In the melee, things in the bar begin to get broken, and Ron calls the sheriff.

The fight is nearly over when Sheriff Richards walks in. "What took place here, Ron?" Sheriff Richards asks.

"Jesse is at it again, Sheriff," Ron replies. "I'm not saying these guys didn't deserve a good whoopin', but I told him I didn't want any trouble in here. You know how Jesse is. He just couldn't let it go, and now look at this place. It's a mess."

"Jesse," Sheriff Richards begins, "I've warned you one too many times, and this time you are going to jail. Come on now and don't give me any trouble."

"They deserved it, Sheriff," Jesse insists in his defense.

"I don't care," Sheriff Richards tells Jesse. "This time you are going to jail, and the judge is going to have to figure out some way to make you understand that this is not how we settle things. Let's go." Sheriff Richards takes Jesse by the arm and escorts him outside to the squad car. He places him in the car and takes him to jail.

Sheriff Richards telephones the Drury ranch, and Carla answers the phone, saying, "Hello."

"Carla?" Sheriff Richards inquires.

"Yes," Carla replies.

"This is Sheriff Richards," the sheriff begins. "I have Jesse in custody. I'm afraid he's gotten into trouble again. This time he is going to have to see Judge Reiber before I can release him."

"What on earth did he do this time, Sheriff?" Carla asks.

"I'm afraid he's been fighting again, and this time he really messed up a couple of guys and broke a lot of stuff in the process," Sheriff Richards tells Carla. "I'm afraid he's really gotten himself into trouble this time. If you want, I will talk to the judge and see what kind of deal I can make, but he has really got to figure out a way to control himself. Chuck Reiber and I have been friends for a long time, but I'm not sure how lenient he will be with Jesse this time. You know it's not the first time he's been in front of Judge Reiber, and the judge doesn't like to see repeat offenders, especially for the same thing that they were in front of him for the last time."

"I know he has been getting out of hand lately," Carla responds, "but Wil and I just don't know what to do anymore, and now Wil is back to drinking. I can't imagine things getting any worse. I just don't know what I am going to do."

"Now don't fret," Sheriff Richards replies. "I'll talk to the judge, and I am pretty sure we can figure out a way to keep him out of jail. He sure likes to fight, and he's good at it. Too bad that's the wrong way to go about things."

"Thank you, Sheriff." Carla sighs. "I'll let Wil know, and we will wait for you to give us a call so we can come down and pick him up."

"Okay," Sheriff Richards states, "I'll call you. Bye now."

"Bye," Carla answers and hangs up the phone.

The next day Sheriff Richards pulls into Drury's driveway, gets out of his squad car, and makes his way to the front door. He is met at the door by Carla.

"Hello, Sheriff," Carla says as she opens the door, "what brings you out this way today?"

"Well," Sheriff Richards begins, "I have news about Jesse and wanted to talk to you in person. Is Wil around?"

"I'm not too sure where he is," Carla responds. "I think it is best if we just go ahead and talk without him."

"If you want," Sheriff Richards replies.

You have news about Jesse?" Carla inquires.

"Yes," Sheriff Richards answers, "and it's gonna take a little explaining."

"Well, let's sit down," Carla says. "Can I get you some coffee?"

"That would be great," Sheriff Richards states.

Carla gets the sheriff a cup of coffee and hands it to him.

"Thanks, Carla," Sheriff Richards says as he accepts the coffee from Carla. "Now the first thing I have to tell you is that Judge Reiber wasn't very receptive to any kind of a deal. He said that Jesse has been in front of him too many times for fighting, and each time it is a little worse than the time before. After he thought about it for a little while, he had a change of heart."

"Meaning you put some pressure on him?" Carla interrupts the sheriff.

"Well, maybe a little," Sheriff Richards admits. "He wouldn't give in much, and that is why I need to talk to you and Wil. You see, the only deal that Judge Reiber is willing to make to keep Jesse out of jail is that he goes into the military. He says it will be a good experience for him, and they will teach him how to control his fighting. He can't get that kind of help in a jail cell."

"Oh dear," Carla sighs. "I wasn't expecting that. I am not sure what Wil will say, and you know, Sheriff, that things are shaping up for this country to get into another war with the Germans again. What does Jesse think of the idea?"

"I haven't talked to Jesse about the deal yet," Sheriff Richards tells Carla. "I wanted to talk to you and Wil first. I will have to tell him when I get back to the station."

"I think we should leave the decision up to Jesse," Carla states. "I will talk to Wil, but I think the best thing we can do at this point is support Jesse with whatever decision he makes. Can you let me know what he decides?"

"Oh sure, Carla," Sheriff Richards responds, "just as soon as I get an answer from Jesse, I'll let you know. Whatever he decides, though, the judge wants him in his courtroom tomorrow, and he will do what he has to do."

"All right, Sheriff," Carla says in agreement, "Wil and I will be there tomorrow, and we will meet with you and Jesse first to discuss his decision."

"Very well then," Sheriff Richards concedes. "Be in my office at 10:00 a.m., and we will all go to the judge's courtroom together."

"Fine, Sheriff," Carla replies, "we will see you at ten tomorrow."

Sheriff Richards stands up, thanks Carla again for the coffee, and leaves.

CHAPTER 7

TOUGH DECISIONS

Carla and Wil arrive at the sheriff's station a little before 10:00 am. Jesse is still being held in a cell. Sheriff Richards is sitting at his desk as Carla and Wil enter his office.

"Have you talked to Jesse, Sheriff?" Carla asks.

"I did," Sheriff Richards replies calmly. "He wanted to know what you and Wil thought, so I decided you two can talk to him together. I will get him, and we can all have a conversation before going to see Judge Reiber." The sheriff gets up from his desk and brings Jesse out of his cell to meet with Wil and Carla.

Although Wil shows no emotion, Carla looks sad as Jesse comes out to meet with them. He pulls up a chair and sits down.

"I guess you all know what this is all about," Jesse begins. "I have kinda made up my mind, but I wanted to hear what you and Uncle Wil have to say."

Carla is unable to control her emotions and cannot speak, but Wil begins, "Well, son, you have learned a great deal living here on the ranch. I know that most of the time the fights you get in, you did not start. No matter, the judge has seen enough of you in his court. I really don't see where anyone has much choice in this matter. I was hoping that I would never have to see you go off into the military. I figured your father and I have paid enough with our service. With any luck, you will be able to serve your time without having to go to war. I don't know, but all in all I think it's the best decision as it's sure as hell a lot better than being locked up in a cell."

"Well," Jesse states, "that does it then. I will go into the army and make the best of it. With any luck, I will come out a better man. Let's go see the judge."

They all stand up and walk out of the sheriff's office and enter the judge's courtroom.

"Sheriff Richards," the judge begins sternly, "has young Mr. Drury been appraised of the situation at hand?"

"He has, Your Honor," Sheriff Richards states.

"Very well then," Judge Reiber replies, "let us begin then. Mr. Drury, I have seen you in my court too many times and were it not for your family's good standing in this community and the insistence of Sheriff Richards, I would see to it that you spend some time behind bars. I explained to Sheriff Richards that I would give you one last chance, but the stipulation would be that in lieu of jail, you enlist in the military. What have you decided?"

Jesse responds to the judge in short, "I have decided that I would rather be under the control of the army than be locked up in a cage."

"Very well then, son," Judge Reiber states, "I will give you ten days to prepare and enlist in the army. If you do not enlist, or if you are brought before my court prior to your enlisting, I will have no choice but to put you in jail for quite some time. Do I make myself clear?"

"Yes, Judge," Jesse answers, "there will be no more trouble, and I will go into the army."

"Very well then," the judge responds, "you are free to go." The judge raps his gavel and leaves the courtroom.

Wil, Carla, and Jesse get up and thank Sheriff Richards, and they all leave the courtroom together. Wil, Carla, and Jesse get into the pickup and head back to the ranch. It is a long quiet ride.

Once they get back to the ranch, Carla goes inside, but Wil tells Jesse there are some things he wants to show him before he goes off to the army.

Jesse follows Wil into the house, and they go to the upstairs. Wil begins to pull things out of the closet and sets them on the floor, revealing a loose board in the back of the closet. "Well, son," Wil tells Jesse, "This is where I keep the rifles, so no one would ever find them. You may need to know where they are someday." Wil reaches into the hiding space and pulls Tall's knife out and hands it to Jesse. "This was your father's, and I want you to take it with you when you go into the army. Your father and I had our knives with us when we went off to war, and we exchanged them right before we went into battle. The knife that your father gave your mother was my knife." Reaching in to get his knife, Wil continues, "You see, they are exactly alike except for our names on the blade."

Jesse closes Tall's knife, sticks it in his pocket, and retreats to his room to prepare for enlisting in the army.

Back in Washington, DC, things are also very much in an uproar. President Roosevelt has been fielding telephone calls from the European Allies who are trying to get the US to get into the war. Winston Churchill is particularly demanding and calling the president every day as things continue to heat up with Germany. Roosevelt isn't ready for the US to get involved in the war, having just finished WWI not that many years ago. The president is attending briefings on an ongoing basis and continually getting updates on the German movement in Europe. The pressure is on.

There is another problem on the horizon for President Roosevelt. The Japanese have been building their military forces with the intention of ruling the Pacific. This is of particular interest to the Australian prime minister, who has also been consulting with Roosevelt.

The Japanese military leaders decide to hold a meeting to confer as to how best to get the US involved in the Pacific. The decision has been made that if the US were to engage in fighting on both the European front and the Pacific front, then the Japanese will have no trouble in defeating the US and controlling the Pacific. They do not believe the US will be able to fight a divided fight. At the meeting, the head Japanese military leader is briefed that the US is very hesitant in getting involved in Europe again, but that Churchill is putting a lot of pressure on the American president to get involved and help to save Europe once again. It is believed that eventually Roosevelt will give in and take up arms in Europe. The question now is how best to also get the US involved in the Pacific.

"Send them and invitation," the head military leader insists.

"By what means?" questions one of the top aides.

"Am I the only one in this room thinking?" the head leader demands.

The rest of the staff look puzzled, and the leader laughs.

"We have been doing studies with the jet stream for a long time now. Why not place bombs on balloons, let them float across the Pacific and land on American soil?" the leader asks. "Is this not possible? At least it is worth a try, is it not?"

"Brilliant," the staff responds.

"Well then," the leader insists. "Get on with it then. It should make some exciting news when the Americans react."

The meeting is adjourned, and the Japanese military prepares and launches the balloon bombs within a few days. A barrage of balloon bombs is sent into the jet stream with hopes that their experiment will succeed, and the bombs will reach the US, thus inviting the US into a war with Japan in the Pacific.

Back in Washington, DC, the president is informed that indeed Japan has launched the bombs, and although most landed in Western Canada, some did reach the Pacific Northwest of the United States. The president immediately put out orders for a news blackout so as not to alarm the American people and to keep the Japanese from finding out that their experiment had worked to some degree.

Jesse is in boot camp now and has had some difficulty with adjusting to the army way of life. He was not accustomed to someone telling him what to do every minute of every day. He did get along eventually and exceeded quite well on the firing range in spite of the fact that all the military rifles are designed for righthanded people. His sergeant took notice of Jesse's skill and accuracy with a rifle and recommended him for the Special Forces team. Jesse wasn't sure if that was what he wanted but decided to give it a try.

He did quite well, and when the opportunity came for him to get advanced training, he embraced it with open arms.

As part of his advanced training, Jesse was required to train with the navy SEALs on a ship in the South Pacific. While on board the ship with the SEALs, the president, enraged by the Japanese balloon bomb incident, instructed his military advisors to have someone look into what was going on with the Japanese and the Australians. It was discovered that Japan was trying to invade mainland Australia, but the Australians were valiantly trying to fend off the invasion by meeting the Japanese on the island of Borneo. The fighting was fierce, and the Australians were taking a beating. The president, still not wanting to get involved in the war with Japan, ordered that one of the special forces personnel be dispatched to the island of Borneo "to have a look around," but he also urged that the US not get directly involved. This assignment was just to Jesse's liking, and he volunteered for the assignment.

While packing his things to prepare for his mission, Jesse went to the ship's supply master and requested several packs of playing cards, which he packed away secretly. He now had everything he needed; a rifle, ammunition, a radio, his father's knife, and the queen of diamonds that his mother had given him, which he tucked into his shirt pocket, remembering that she had told him to always carry it with him to keep him safe.

CHAPTER 8

THE WAR

The SEAL team departs from the mother ship in order to deliver Jesse to the island under the cover of darkness. Although none of the SEALs wear any rank insignia, everyone knew who the leader of the team was. It was Captain Brian Erickson, a straightforward, no-nonsense type of guy and an excellent team leader.

The team reaches the shore of the island in the middle of the night. As Jesse is stepping out onto the shore, he is addressed by Captain Erickson.

"Jesse," the captain commands, "now remember, your orders are to look around and report back as to your findings. You are to remain undetected, and we will pick you up back here in two weeks. Be waiting on shore at this spot about midnight. You are to observe radio silence unless there is an emergency. On board the ship, we will be monitoring the radio waves. We will have no way to contact you should an unforeseen situation arise whereby we would be unable to complete the rendezvous. Good luck."

And with that, the two shake hands, Jesse disappears into the night, and the SEAL team drifts back out into the ocean.

Jesse's first order of business is to check out the layout of the island. In doing so, Jesse discovers a narrow passage that he dubs the Hole in the Wall. As he ventures further beyond the "Wall," Jesse discovers a Japanese encampment, and with that discovery, Jesse decides it is best for him to keep the Wall between his camp and the Japanese.

Everything is going fine for Jesse as he covers the island and gathers information to take back to the ship. As he discovers certain points of interest, Jesse pins on a tree near his vantage point four cards: two black aces and two black eights. At one particular vantage point, Jesse has discovered a pair of machine gun nests meant to catch the encroaching enemy in a crossfire. Just as Jesse is about to leave his position, he sees in the distance a group of soldiers headed straight toward the machine gun nests. As the group nears, Jesse can see that these are Australian soldiers, and they are headed into an ambush.

Although his orders were that he remain undetected, Jesse cannot stand by and allow the Australians to walk blindly into an ambush. There is only one way to warn them, and that is to take out the gunners in the nests. With careful aim, Jesse takes out the most distant one and then the closer one—two shots, two kills. The Aussies are alerted, and as they continue, they can see what has happened, but they are confused as to who the shooter may have been, so without delay, they retreat back to their camp to try and get an understanding of the situation. They are, however, grateful for the warning.

The shots were also heard back at the Japanese encampment, and troops are dispatched to find out what has happened. They come upon the machine gun nests with the dead gunners. They spread out in all directions to find the shooter. The first group discovers that the Australian troops had been close by, but there is no spent ammunition. Another group comes upon Jesse's vantage point, and they find the cards tacked to a tree.

Removing the cards, they return to the camp and report to the commander, who orders them to return and find the shooter.

Fearing that he may be followed, Jesse is in position at the hole in the wall. As the Japanese approach, they must go single file through the passage. Just as Jesse planned it, he begins taking out the Japanese soldiers one by one until they retreat.

"So much for remaining undetected," Jesse whispers to himself.

When the Japanese soldiers return with the news of the ambush, the commander is extremely upset. He is sure that the shooter left the cards, but what is their meaning?

The commander orders an all-out manhunt for the shooter, which leads to confrontations nearly every day, with Jesse making his escape through the hole in the wall. Knowing he is a hunted man now; Jesse decides that he will spend the rest of his time at his vantage point above the hole in the wall until the SEAL team arrives to pick him up.

Unknown to Jesse, during his absence at the hole in the wall, the Japanese have placed artillery, which they will use to bombard the shooter the next time he tries to defend the hole in the wall.

As Jesse is out scouting the island this morning, he hears an aircraft coming toward the island. Jesse watches intently as the plane makes a low approach over the ocean and then pulls up as it nears the island. The pilot had no way of knowing that Jesse was on the island on a top-secret mission. The pilot circles several times, taking photographs of the island. The Japanese, too, spot the aircraft and quickly identify it as an American plane, and they hurry to man their guns.

In an instant, the Japanese guns open up, and the aircraft is hit. The pilot tries to make it back out to sea to crash the plane but is unable to fly that far. The plane is on fire and going down fast as the pilot ejects.

Jesse watches carefully, marking the spot where the plane will crash and where the pilot will land. He scrambles to reach the site. He must get to the pilot before the Japanese do.

As Jesse nears the downed pilot, he can see that the man waited too long to eject, and his chute did not completely deploy. The pilot is badly burned and injured, Jesse notes as he unstraps him from his parachute and seat. The pilot is unconscious but alive. Jesse knows that time is short, and he must get the pilot to safety. Jesse looks through the rubble until he finds the emergency locator beacon. He stashes the beacon in his shirt, sends out an SOS on his own radio, and loads the pilot on his back. Jesse knows he must make it to the hole in the wall before the Japanese catch up to him and the pilot. There is no time to delay.

Jesse reaches the hole in the wall well ahead of the Japanese but knows that they will be coming. He must get the pilot to the rendezvous point to meet up with the recovery team, so he packs up the pilot again, and off they go.

Jesse stays hidden just offshore, awaiting the recovery team.

The pilot regains consciousness during their wait.

"Okay now, Captain," Jesse begins, "you are going to be just fine. What is your name?"

The captain moans. "Jack. What is yours?"

"I'm Jesse," Jesse responds, "and I'm going to get you out of here."

"Where are you from, Jesse?" the pilot asks.

"A little town in Wyoming that nobody has ever heard of," Jesse replies.

"Well, it must have a name," the captain demands.

"Barnum. Barnum, Wyoming," Jesse says with a laugh. "Now I bet you never heard of that town, Captain."

The captain shakes his head no.

"Okay now, Captain," Jesse begins, but is interrupted by the captain.

"Please, call me Jack," the captain asks.

"Okay, Jack," Jesse continues, "I have to be getting back to the Hole in the Wall to thwart off the Japanese until the recovery team gets here."

"You are just going to leave me here?" Jack asks.

"I have placed the locator beacon here with you, and the recovery team will find you. You will be fine, as long as I can hold off the Japs," Jesse sternly tells Jack.

"And then you will come out with us?" Jack asks.

"No," Jesse answers, "they will send another team for me later. Right now, we must get you out of here. There is something you can do for me, Jack."

"Just name it, Jesse," Jack states.

Jesse reaches into his pocket and takes out his knife. Then he reaches into another pocket and retrieves a letter that he has written and addressed to Carla. "Here, Jack," Jesse says. "Just in case, I want you to get these to my parents in Barnum, Wyoming. I know you will be able to find it. It's not much of a town."

"So just like that you are going to leave me here?" Jack asks worriedly.

"Look, Jack," Jesse answers sharply, "we have already discussed that. If you are worried, then here." Jesse reaches into his shirt pocket and takes out the queen of diamonds. "Here," Jesse begins again, placing the card in Jack's pocket, "this is the closest thing my mother had to a picture of her. She said to keep it with me, and it would keep me safe. I am giving it to you so that you will get back safely. I have to go now."

"But what will keep you safe?" Jack asks Jesse.

Jesse pulls up his shirt and reveals his aces and eights tattoo. Jesse then turns and heads back to his vantage point at the hole in the wall. Jesse looks back one last time and says to Jack, "Just make sure my parents get my knife and letter."

Jesse can see the recovery team approaching, and he knows that Jack will be fine as he disappears into the jungle.

Jesse is in position to thwart off the Japanese if they try to get through the hole in the wall. At the same time, the recovery team has reached Jack, loaded him in the raft, and set back out to sea.

Jesse is puzzled at the fact that the Japanese have not yet tried to advance through the hole in the wall. From his vantage point, he can see that the recovery team is headed back out to sea. He waits now, but not for long. He gets a glimpse of the first Japanese soldier coming through the hole in the wall. Jesse takes aim and dispatches the soldier, but he was not ready for what would happen next.

The Japanese now have Jesse's position and fire off a barrage of artillery. The shells are landing all around, and there is no escape for Jesse this time.

Jack was lying on his back in the raft when the recovery team hears the artillery. Jack sits up quickly to see what is going on. There is no question that Jesse is being bombarded. Many shots are fired, and there is smoke and fire everywhere near Jesse's position. Jack falls on his back and mumbles a prayer of thanks to Jesse for saving his life. He knows that Jesse will not make it off the island, and he now realizes that Jesse, too, knew that.

"I'll make my report when we get back," Captain Erickson tells Jack, "that our man on the island gave his all so that our mission would be successful."

CHAPTER 9

CAPTURED

Although the recovery team was sure that Jesse had been killed in the firefight that took place, he, in fact, had not been killed. He had been captured by the Japanese.

Jesse, injured in the attack, is marched into the Japanese commander's office.

"Well," the Japanese commander begins, "what do we have here? I don't believe that you are Australian now, are you?" Looking over Jesse's rifle, the commander continues, "This is not an Australian rifle. No, this is an American rifle." He holds the rifle up to his shoulder, "Yes, and a fine rifle it is. It will be nice to have it in my collection. Now just what is an American doing on this island? And I see that your right hand has been badly injured. Oh well, you will not be doing any more shooting anyway."

Jesse remains silent.

"So, you don't want to talk," the Japanese commander continues. "Shu, is my tea ready yet?" the commander barks at his houseboy. "And now back to you," the commander says as he reaches for Jesse's dog tags and tears them from his neck. "Here, Shu, a souvenir," the commander says as he hands Shu the dog tags and accepts his cup of tea. The commander throws the scalding hot tea into Jesse's right eye, "Oh yes, you will not be needing your shooting eye anymore either. What is it that you Americans say? Take an eye, give an eye?" The commander laughs.

Jesse uses his left hand to take his shirt to wipe his eye, revealing his aces and eights tattoo.

"So," the commander says as he notices Jesse's tattoo, "it is indeed you who has left all these calling cards of aces and eights. Do they have any particular meaning?"

Still, Jesse remains silent.

"Okay," the commander says with a laugh, "we will see how long you can remain silent. We have some treatments here to make people talk. We will see if you are as strong as a common houseboy. Shu, come here and roll up your sleeve."

Shu does as the commander says, as the commander lights a cigarette. His arm reveals several cigarettes burn scars and a crossed swords tattoo. After taking a couple of puffs, the commander puts out his cigarette on Shu's arm, but Shu does not even flinch.

"There, you see," the commander says to Jesse. "Here even a boy is taught to not show any feelings or emotions. We shall see if the Americans are taught this also. Get him out of here. I need to make my report to headquarters."

With that, Jesse is ushered outside and placed in a cell, which is nothing more than a cage, but every day Jesse is brought to the commander's office, seated in a chair while the commander places one bullet in his revolver and gives it a spin. Shu is forced to watch as the commander asks Jesse if today his lucky day is, places the revolver to Jesse's head, and pulls the trigger.

Shu repaired Jesse's dog tag chain and wears it around his neck. He is intrigued by Jesse and slowly gets closer to Jesse's cage day by day.

The commander has made his report to headquarters stating that an American has been captured on the island and that the American has shot several Japanese soldiers here on the island.

The head military leader for Japan is angered at the receipt of the report from the Japanese commander, and he calls in his military team. "Gentlemen," the leader begins, "it appears that the Americans are giving some thought to entering the war. We have captured an American on the island of Borneo, apparently trying to assist the Australians in reclaiming the island. I believe it is time we sent the Americans another invitation to join the war." The leader pulls down a map and points to Hawaii. "Here," the leader states, "is the closest American naval base. I want a full squadron of kamikaze pilots sent to this base and inflict as much damage as is possible. The Americans will never be expecting us, and certainly this will convince them to join the war."

The meeting is dismissed, and the squadron of kamikazes strikes Pearl Harbor, propelling the United States into WWII.

Upon hearing the news of the strike on Pearl Harbor, Japanese admiral Isoroku Yamamoto states, "I fear all we have done is to awaken a sleeping giant and fill him with a terrible resolve."

Shu has now become more comfortable with Jesse, and he delivers the news to him that the United States has entered the war.

"How do you know that?" Jesse asks.

"Japan has made an air raid on the US naval port of Pearl Harbor, and the US has declared war on Japan," Shu tells Jesse.

"Why do you let him torture you, Shu?" Jesse questions.

"I belong to him," Shu says as he pulls up his sleeve and shows Jesse the burned in crossed swords tattoo of ownership, "and I must do whatever he asks of me."

"Why don't you just shoot him in the middle of the night and be done with him?" Jesse continues.

"Oh," Shu states, "I could never do anything like that. I want to help people, not hurt them, no matter what they have done to me. Someday I hope to be a doctor and help many people."

"Well," Jesse says, "if I get the chance, I will kill him for you."

Shu looks at Jesse and says, "If I ever get the chance, I will help you escape."

"You know, Shu," Jesse begins, "you and I have just made a promise to each other, and a promise made is a debt unpaid. I hope someday you will get the chance to show me you mean what you say. Either way, if I ever get the chance, I will kill him for you, or maybe for both of us."

Shu looks to the ground and then turns and walks away.

As the days pass, the Australians have mustered up their troops with the intent of taking back the island of Borneo. Upon hearing word of the intended Australian assault, the Japanese leader issues orders to evacuate the island and leave no prisoners behind.

The commander, having received the orders to evacuate, walks out to Jesse's cage with his pistol in one hand and a deck of cards in the other. "Well, my American friend," the commander addresses Jesse, "it would seem that the time has come for us to go our separate ways. I am afraid today is not your lucky day. You have done well, and I will make this as quick as possible."

The commander raises his pistol and pulls the trigger, hitting Jesse in the head. He then tosses the deck of cards onto Jesse's fallen body and says, "There, my American friend, you may rest with your cards."

The commander signals his troops to depart as Shu looks back to Jesse with a tear in his eye, in spite of being conditioned to never show emotion.

Jesse's life is slowly fading away, and he flashes back to the scene when his mother left him at the orphanage. "I want to go with you, Momma. Please let me go with you," Jesse begs over and over.

"No, son," Memory says to Jesse, "you cannot go with me. You must stay here. I love you more than anything in this world, Jesse, but you cannot go with me."

The queen of diamonds has fallen into Jesse's left hand, and unconsciously he grasps it as the fight is going on in his head between his mother and him. Jesse desperately wants to go with his mother, but she insists that it is not his time. He cannot go with her. He must stay.

CHAPTER 10

RECOVERY

While Jesse is in the custody of the Japanese, the pilot, Jack, is sent back to the United States for medical treatment, but after a medical evaluation, he is given a medical discharge from the military.

Jack decides to go to Arizona until he can fully recover. He has political connections in the northeast, and he calls his brother, who is a United States senator.

"Ted," Jack says into the phone, "I want you to do something for me. The soldier who saved my life, his name is Jesse James, I want you to pull his military records and see to it that he is awarded the Medal of Honor. I have some things that he gave me to be returned to his parents in Wyoming, and I also want to give them their son's Medal of Honor. I would not be here if it were not for him. Can you do that for me, Ted? Okay then, let me know when you get it done."

As Jack slowly recovers, he decides to visit the Phoenix Art Museum. He walks slowly around the museum assisted by a cane. He does not pause long until he sees a pen-and-ink drawing done by Fredric Remington. He is taken by the drawing. It is a picture of a stagecoach being pursued by what appears to be a group of bandits. A lone man with a rifle has exited the coach and is standing in the trail with his rifle aimed at the bandits. Jack mumbles to himself as he reads the title of the drawing, *They Left Him Thar in the Trail.* Jack continues to stare at the drawing, but in actuality, he is thinking back to his own rescue. The scene with Jesse leaving him to be rescued, while Jesse goes back to thwart off the pursuing Japanese soldiers, flashes through his mind. Then quietly, Jack exits the museum.

Jack returns to the museum every day and goes directly to the Remington drawing, where he stands and stares for quite a long while.

The curator notices that Jack comes to the museum every day, but only views one picture. Quietly, the curator approaches Jack and speaks to him, "You know, we have many other paintings in this museum, but I see that you are particularly attracted to this one. May I ask what it is about this drawing that so captivates you?"

Jack is a bit taken when he hears the curator's voice, but responds, "Oh, it's not really anything in particular. I was just thinking of how it would look hanging in my office."

The curator smiles. "The only office this drawing would ever hang in would be the Oval Office, so unless you are the president of the United States, I don't think there is much chance that this drawing will ever hang in your office."

"Yes, of course," Jack replies. "Well, it was worth a thought." Jack walks away from the curator without saying another word and exits the museum.

The Medal of Honor for Jesse is sent to Jack in Arizona. Now he has everything that he wanted to deliver to Jesse's parents in Wyoming, and Jack prepares for his trip to visit Jesse's family.

Jack makes the trip to Wyoming and stops in Kaycee to get directions to Jesse's parents' ranch. He sees the sheriff's office and decides to try there. As Jack walks into Sheriff Richards's office, he sees the sheriff sitting at his desk looking over paperwork. Looking up to see who has entered, Sheriff Richards asks, "May I help you?"

"I hope so," Jack replies. "My name is Jack, and I am looking for a family that lives in Barnum."

"And what is your business with this family?" the sheriff asks. "We don't get many strangers coming through here looking for people in Barnum. There aren't many families out there."

"Well, Sheriff," Jack responds, reaching into his pocket and pulling out Jesse's letter, "I am looking for the Drury family. I made the acquaintance of their son, Jesse, and he asked me to deliver this letter and some other things to his parents."

Jack hands the letter to Sheriff Richards, who looks the letter over carefully.

"This must be pretty important if you are delivering a letter in person," Sheriff Richards answers. "You know we do have postal service here in Wyoming."

"Yes," Jack says, nodding his head, "but I'm afraid that this is something I must do in person. I promised that I would."

"Okay then," Sheriff Richards says, handing the letter back to Jack, "it just so happens that I have business out that way. You can follow me to the Drury ranch."

The sheriff gets up from his desk, puts on his hat, and walks out to his patrol car as Jack follows him.

The sheriff and Jack arrive at the Drury ranch. Carla steps out onto the porch as the vehicles come to a stop. Sheriff Richards gets out of his car and approaches Carla.

"Nice of you to pay us a visit, Dale," Carla says. "To what do we owe this honor?"

The sheriff motions to Jack to come on and says to Carla, "Well, this young man stopped by my office and wanted directions to your place. He has some things for you and Wil. I thought I had better escort him."

"What kind of things?" Carla asks.

"You had better get Wil," the sheriff tells Carla, "And I will let him explain all that to you."

Carla finds Wil in the barn repairing some tack. "Wil," Carla calls, "Dale Richards is here with someone who wants to talk to us."

"What about?" Wil asks curtly.

"I really don't know," Carla says, "but if the sheriff is involved, we had better go and see what he has to say."

"All right," Wil replies, lays down his tools, and walks back to the house with Carla.

Sheriff Richards and Jack are waiting on the porch as Carla and Wil walk up.

"What is this all about, Dale?" Wil questions sternly.

"I think I better answer that," Jack begins. "My name is Jack," Jack says, extending his hand to Wil. "I have some things here that I promised to deliver to you."

"Promised who?" Wil interrupts.

"This is not easy for me," Jack continues. "My plane was downed on the island of Borneo. I tried to get the plane out to sea so the Japanese would not be able to get to the wreckage. I waited as long as I possibly could to eject, which was nearly too late. I was injured badly, but I was rescued by a soldier who was on the island doing reconnaissance work. He took me through a place he called the Hole in the Wall and said it was named after a place where he grew up."

Carla speaks out, "Oh my god, Jesse!"

"Yes," Jack replies, "Jesse James. He didn't tell me much because we didn't have much time. He dropped me off at the rendezvous point and left the locator beacon with me so the recovery team could find me. He said he needed to get back to the Hole in the Wall because he would be able to hold off the Japanese there until the team could pick me up and get me safely back out to sea, but before he left me, he gave me some things." Jack reaches into a large envelope that he had been holding. He pulls out the knife and says, "He first gave me this and said it was his father's and asked that I deliver it back to his family. "

Wil reaches out to receive the knife from Jack. He opens the blade and sees Tall's name on the knife. He then closes the knife and puts it in his pocket. "Yes," Wil says, "it was my brother's knife. Our grandfather made one for each of us when we went off to World War I. What else do you have?"

Jack again reaches into the envelope and says, "He wanted me to deliver this letter. It is addressed to you, ma'am." Jack hands the letter to Carla.

She takes it without saying a word, folds it in half, and places it into her apron pocket.

"He also gave me this playing card," Jack goes on. "He said something about it keeping me safe, that his mother had given it to him to keep him safe. It is badly worn, but it's the queen of diamonds."

Knowing what all this means, Wil says to Jack, "You keep the card, son. Yes, it was Jesse's, but I guess he has no need of it now, and perhaps it will have some meaning for you through the years."

Jack places the card in his shirt pocket and continues, "I was rescued, and as we set back out to sea, there was terrible gunfire and explosions. Jesse was never heard from again. He gave his life to save mine. "I have one more thing," Jack says, reaching into his coat pocket, pulling out a box, and opening it to show Wil and Carla the contents. "Your son was awarded the Medal of Honor, and I am very proud and humbled to give this to you."

Carla is in tears and goes into the house. Wil accepts the medal and says a simple, "Thank you." Wil also goes into the house.

Sheriff Richards turns to Jack and says, "Well, son, you have done what you came here to do. I suppose we had both be on our way now and give these people some time to deal with all this. I want you to stop back by my office and give me all your contact information for my file. I have no doubt that eventually, these folks will want to contact you."

With no further words, Sheriff Richards and Jack get into their vehicles and head back to Kaycee.

CHAPTER 11

RESCUED

Jesse is still alive, but badly injured as the Australians discover the Japanese encampment and search for living prisoners.

"Over here, Sergeant," one of the Australian soldiers hollers out as he sees Jesse's body in the cage.

"Well," the sergeant, Mick Reichle, commands, "don't just stand there. Get in there and bring him out."

The Australian soldiers enter Jesse's cage, bring him out, and place him on the ground. The queen of diamonds is clutched in his left hand.

"He's still warm," Sergeant Reichle says as he touches Jesse's body.

Jesse moans, and the sergeant exclaims, "He's still alive! Get the medics!"

One of the soldiers questions the sergeant, "Do we know who he is, Sergeant?"

"No, Private," Sergeant Reichle states, "but we were sent here to recover all of the soldiers that we can. This one is still alive, and perhaps he will be able to tell us what happened here."

"But we don't even know that he is one of us," the private responds.

"Well, he certainly isn't Japanese now, is he?" Sergeant Reichle responds. "And there are only Japanese and Australians on the island, so that should narrow it down, don't you think?"

The private nods his head in agreement while the sergeant reaches into his pocket. The sergeant pulls out a set of dog tags, places them around Jesse's neck, and says, "Well, we know who he is now, don't we, Private?"

"So, who is he?" the private asks.

"Why, he's Erich Blanton," Sergeant Reichle replies, "and I'm glad we found him."

"But don't you think anyone will be wondering what happened to the real Erich Blanton?" the private questions.

"I doubt it," Sergeant Reichle states boldly. "Erich was a good friend of mine, and I got to know him well. We grew up in an orphanage together. Neither one of us was ever adopted, and we stuck together our whole lives. He even enlisted in the army with me. Neither of us has any family other than each other. He died saving my life, and I have carried his dog tags with me ever since. What's funny is that he always said he wanted a Viking funeral. I promised him that if he went before me, I would see to it that he gets one, and that's exactly what I did, at least as best I could. I built a wooden raft, put a sail on it, set it on fire, and sent him out to sea. Damn, that was hard."

Jesse is taken by the Australian soldiers back to Australia, where he receives medical treatment for his various wounds. With the Australian dog tags around his neck, everyone refers to Jesse as Erich Blanton.

After several days, Jesse regains consciousness, but has difficulty speaking and has no idea of who he is or what happened to him.

Jesse's nurse speaks to him to comfort him, "You are back home now, Erich. You were injured in the war, and you are now in the hospital recovering. Your fellow soldiers brought you in, and they will be glad to find out that you are awake. I will be caring for you. You have a terrible head injury, and I will be teaching you to speak, walk, and get back to a normal life. My name is Carolyn, Carolyn Potts."

So, Jesse, now Erich Blanton, is a native Australian. Erich's wounds heal, but he never regains any memory of what his life was like prior to waking up in the hospital. His speech is very Australian, considering the accent he listened to and learned during speech therapy. He is discharged from the Australian army and begins civilian life as an Australian. His friend and fellow soldier, Mick Reichle, helps him get a job working on a cattle ranch.

Erich seems to adapt to ranching quite quickly. He enjoys working with horses and cattle. Occasionally he will be doing something on the ranch and will get a flashback that he doesn't understand. His life flashes back to another time, another person on another ranch somewhere. It is a short experience but very troubling to Erich, and he yearns to know more about his former life. He contacts his friend Mick to find out how much he knows. Mick can only tell him what life was like with the real Erich Blanton, but he never lets on to Jesse that he is not the real Erich Blanton. When Mick tells Jesse about them growing up in the orphanage together, Jesse gets another flashback of being in an orphanage, but he doesn't see Mick, and he begins to think that there is a lot more to the story.

One day, while attending a rodeo, Erich meets a beautiful rodeo cowgirl. He is immediately taken with her and introduces himself.

"Hello," Erich starts, "my name is Erich Blanton. What is yours?"

A bit surprised, the cowgirl turns around and says, "Why, I'm Jenny, Jenny Gordon. I don't think I have ever seen you before."

"Well, Jenny Gordon," Erich continues, "you have seen me now. Would you sit and watch the rest of the rodeo with me?"

"So, what event do you do?" Jenny asks.

"I don't rodeo yet," Erich responds. "I work on a ranch out south of town. I was injured in the war with the Japanese, but I am recovering just fine. I have some friends who are going to help me get started in rodeo. I am hoping to ride bulls."

"I hope I get to watch you ride bulls some time," Jenny tells Erich.

"Oh, you will," Erich replies.

"Well, I'll be watching for you," Jenny replies, "but right now I have to go. Perhaps I will see you another time."

"You can bet on that," Erich says assuredly, and they go their separate ways. Erich watches as Jenny walks away and whispers to himself, "You can bet on that."

Back at the ranch, Erich begs the other cowboys to help get him to start riding bulls. He finally convinces one of the older cowboys, Don Mitchell, to show him how to ride bulls.

Don and Erich load a couple of bulls into the chutes on the ranch. Erich looks over at Don and says, "Thanks, Don, I really appreciate this."

Don responds, "Maybe you had better wait until after your first ride or so to thank me. I hope you know what you are getting yourself in for."

Erich smiles and answers Don, "You just tell me what to do, and I will do all the rest."

Don explains to Erich what he needs to do. They put a rope on the first bull, and Erich was excited to buck out of the chute. Erich gets on his bull while Don is waiting to open the gate. "Nod when you think you are ready and then hold on," Don tells Erich.

Erich smiles and nods. The bull comes out of the chute, bucking hard. Erich goes flying off the back end of the bull and lands on the ground flat on his back. He has the wind knocked out of him, and he just lies in the arena trying to catch his breath. The bull spots Erich and makes a run at him, but Don grabs Erich, jerks him to his feet, and pulls him to the fence, where they both jump up as high as they can to get away from the bull. Don lectures Erich, "Boy, once you are off that beast, you got to get to your feet and head for the fence. Those critters will stomp the shit out of you if they get the chance."

Erich instantly has a flashback to when his uncle said the same thing to him on the ranch in Wyoming.

"Thanks, Don," Erich says, gasping for air, "that was fuckin' fun. Come on and let's load up another one."

Don just smiles and nods okay. "I'll say this much for you, you sure don't have any quit in ya," Don tells Erich.

Erich smiles and replies, "Not one bit. Let's go."

After some intense practice sessions, Erich excels in bull riding, and he is ready for his first rodeo. So, he enters a local "jackpot" rodeo, and who else is there but Jenny Gordon.

"Hello, Jenny," Erich says, sneaking up behind her.

"Well," Jenny says as she turns around, "I saw you were entered in the bull riding. I'll be watching you."

Erich nods his head, smiles, and walks away. As luck would have it, Erich draws a good bull and wins the rodeo. Of course, Jenny was cheering for him the whole ride. They meet up after the rodeo, and Erich talks Jenny into a dinner date. From that point on, the two begin seeing each other on a regular basis.

CHAPTER 12

REMEMBERING

Erich is having the time of his life, working on the ranch, going to rodeos, and dating Jenny, but each day he seems to remember things about his past.

Barely a year passes as Jenny and Erich are married and remain on the ranch. Jenny does the cooking and cleaning while Erich sees to his ranch duties. It is a good fit for both of them, and they get to spend a lot of time together. Within two years, Addison Grace is born, but there are soon to be problems on the horizon. Erich is remembering more and more every day, and he begins to picture the ranch in Wyoming and other pieces of his past.

Erich approaches Jenny with his problems and says, "Jenny, you know I love you, and I want only the best for you and our little Addi, but the past has really been haunting me lately. I have put a lot of pieces together, and I have decided that I must go back to the US and find my past."

"And what is to become of Addi and me?" Jenny asks, crying.

"Jenny," Erich says sternly, "I need to find out who I really am and where I come from. Once I have done that, I will return here to you and Addi. I could never leave you. Please believe me."

Jenny turns her back on Erich and walks away.

Erich prepares for his trip to America and looks forward to finding out his true past. For the most part his trip is uneventful, but all that changes as his bus ride takes him through Wyoming. He remembers being in Cheyenne, although he is not really sure how he got there or why he was there. He looks around, and many things look familiar. As the bus ventures north toward Casper, Erich recalls seeing much of the scenery before, and he recalls going to Kaycee and staying with the sheriff. He has flashbacks of his pack, the knife, the dime novels, and the card, the queen of diamonds. He has a flashback of his mother giving him the card to keep him safe, but then he sees himself handing the card to someone else. All this is very puzzling to him.

Erich, now back in Kaycee, Wyoming, tries desperately to find his past. He is unsure of what to do, but since he remembered staying with the sheriff, he decides to pay the sheriff a visit. Walking through the door of the sheriff's office, Erich says, "Hello there, Sheriff, so how is your day going?"

Sheriff Richards looks up from his desk. He is puzzled as to who the stranger is. "What can I do for you?" Sheriff Richards asks.

"Well, sir," Erich begins, "I think I grew up somewhere around here, and I was maybe hoping that you could point me in the right direction."

"So, what is your name, and why can't you remember where you grew up?" Sheriff Richards questions Erich.

"You see, Sheriff," Erich continues, "I was injured on the island of Borneo, where I was captured by the Japanese and rescued by the Australians. I had total memory loss, so the Australians took me in and helped me along. They said I was one of them, but then I keep getting flashbacks of growing up here in Wyoming, and I am trying to put the pieces together."

"I see," Sheriff Richards replies, "and what is it that you think I can do for you? You know, you still haven't told me your name. We should probably start with that."

"Right now, I am called Erich Blanton, from Australia," Erich tells the sheriff, "But as I said, that is the name the Australians gave me. I am not sure what my real name is or how I can find out, but I do have a recollection of staying in this jail at one time in my life, which is why I came to talk to you."

Sheriff Richards gets a blank stare on his face as he thinks back to years gone by. He looks at Erich and asks, "You say you stayed in the jail. Why, did you do something wrong?"

Erich replies, "That's just it, Sheriff, I don't know why I stayed in the jail, but somehow my mind says that I did. I don't think I did anything wrong, because all the flashbacks show that I was not very old at the time, like maybe ten or so. The only other thing I can tell you is that it seems that all I had on me was a backpack with a pocketknife, some paperback books, and a playing card. It was the queen of diamonds."

Scratching his head, Sheriff Richards tells Erich, "You know, there was a time when I had a young man here in the jail. That was a long time ago. That can't be who you are, though, because he was killed in the war. I guess I never did hear exactly where he was when he was killed." Beginning to suspect something, Sheriff Richards pulls his gun and says to Erich, "Now just maybe you met this guy, and you know he was killed, and now you are coming back here to possibly collect on any money or property he had. I remember that the knife he had with him during the war was returned to his family. Let's go, in the cell until I can get all this stuff figured out." And with that being said, Erich is locked up by Sheriff Richards. Sheriff Richards checks Erich for weapons but doesn't find any. Erich is very cooperative. "Look, Erich, or whoever you are," Sheriff Richards says as he puts on his hat, "I have got to go and get some information and run a check on you. I'll be back after a while, and if you check out, you will be free to go."

"So, you have information about my past?" Erich asks.

"I didn't say that," Sheriff Richards responds as he is walking out the door.

Sheriff Richards remembered that the boy he had locked up in his jail several years ago had been adopted by Wil and Carla Drury. He thought about the fact that the boy, Jesse, had gotten into a lot of trouble and was sent off to the military by Judge Reiber. The problem now was that the Drury ranch had sat vacant now for several years. Wil Drury had died, and Carla was in a nursing home. There was no other choice but to go and talk to her. The problem was, what would he tell her? Certainly, she would want to know why he was asking her about their son. He would need to have some answers for her, but he didn't want to tell her about the man he had locked up in the jail. Perplexed,

Sheriff Richards talked to himself while he was driving his squad car to the nursing home.

Sheriff Richards pulls into the parking lot of the nursing home, still not sure of what he is going to say to Carla. As Sheriff Richards walks through the door, Carla has her back to him, looking out a window. Quietly Sheriff Richards calls to Carla, "Carla, how are you today?"

Carla turns and says, "Why, Dale, I'm fine, thank you. What brings you here?"

"Well," Dale begins, "I'm not really sure. You see, Carla, I have a man in my jail that claims he was injured in the war and lost his memory. He claims that it is slowly coming back and that he remembers growing up around here."

"Do you think it is my Jesse?" Carla interrupts.

"I'm just not sure," Dale tells her. "He could have been in the service with your Jesse, and Jesse told him all about growing up here, and now he is trying to horn in on Jesse's inheritance or something. I don't know. It just doesn't seem right. You remember that man that brought you Jesse's things and said he was killed, don't you?"

"So, Dale," Carla asks, "just what does he remember? You know that I have had several conversations with Jack since the day he was here, and there was never any proof that Jesse was killed. I still don't believe he was killed, and I have been waiting for him to come home. Can I go see him?"

"I knew you were going to want to do that, Carla," Dale tells her, "And I really didn't want to get your hopes up. This guy talks with a really strong accent of some kind, like English or Australian."

Again, Carla, with wide eyes, interrupts Dale, "Did you say he has an Australian accent?"

"Well, it's something like that. Why?" Dale asks.

Carla answers Dale, "Don't you remember when that man brought Jesse's things to Wil and me that he told us that he had crashed his plane on the island of Borneo? The United States was not engaged in the war at that time, and no American soldiers were to be on Borneo, but Jesse was on Borneo. Jack said Jesse was gathering intelligence about the Japanese that were trying to invade mainland Australia. It is very possible that Jesse was not killed, but captured and then rescued by the Australians when they took back Borneo. If he could not identify himself at the time, they would have assumed that he was Australian and would have taken him back to Australia with them. Don't you see, Dale? This could very easily be my Jesse. I want to go see him now. I will know if it is him. Let's go now."

Carla goes to her room and takes some things out of her dresser drawer and places them into her purse. The two depart and head for the sheriff's office. Once they arrive, Carla does not wait for Dale, but hurries into the jailhouse. The minute Jesse sees her, he is sure he knows her, and his eyes light up.

Carla nearly faints when she sees Jesse, but gathers herself and says, "Jesse? It is you, isn't it, Jesse? Is it really you? They told me you were dead, but I refused to believe it."

"You call me Jesse, but my name from Australia is Erich," Jesse replies. "Who told you I was dead?"

"A man showed up here and told Wil and me that you had been killed," Carla answers, reaching into her purse. "He gave me this letter and some other things and said you asked him to bring them to us. Perhaps Erich is the name you have been given by the Australians, but this is your home, and I raised you as Jesse. I'm glad you are home now. We have much to talk about. Dale says you don't remember a lot of what happened to you, and you are searching for answers."

"Yes," Jesse responds, "I keep having flash backs of different things that happened to me, and slowly but surely my memory is coming back."

"Wil has passed away, Jesse," Carla states with tears in her eyes, "and you are all I have left. I knew you were still alive and would come home to me. They have taken me off the ranch and put me in a nursing home. Please, son, take me back home."

"Now just wait a minute, Carla," Dale states sternly, "I can't just let this guy take you back to the ranch. We need to be sure of who he is before I let him out of here."

"You think I don't know that this is Jesse?" Carla says, turning to Dale. "I raised him from a small boy. Wil and I took him in and raised him as our own son. Did you not see that he recognized me right away? What more proof do you want? You were the one who got my boy sent off to war, and now you don't believe he has returned. Wait, I know! Jesse, don't you have a tattoo on your chest? Aces and eights, correct? I never liked it, but perhaps now it will be the proof Dale needs to set you free. Open your shirt and show it to Dale."

Very slowly, as if there were no tattoo there, Jesse unbuttons his shirt while Dale watches with anticipation. Then in one swift move, and without a word, Jesse throws open his left side, revealing the tattoo. Dale looks at it, amazed, and says, "Well I'll be damned." He lets Jesse out of his cell, and Jesse gives Carla a big hug.

"Will you give us a ride out to the ranch, Dale?" Carla asks. "We have much work to do to get things back in order, and now my son is home."

Dale nods that he will take Carla and Jesse to the ranch. He grabs his hat, and they all walk out the door together.

Jesse and Carla are settling back into Wyoming ranch life. Jesse continues to remember his past, but also remembers that he has a wife and daughter in Australia. He writes several letters to Jenny and Addi as he prepares for them to come to America to be with him and live on the ranch. He tells Jenny about all the things he is remembering, including his name as Jesse James and not Erich Blanton.

One morning as Jesse is having breakfast, he picks up a copy of the newspaper and is shocked by what he sees on the front page. It is a picture of the Japanese diplomat who will be coming to the US to meet with the president. Jesse stares at the picture and has a vivid flashback of being held prisoner in the Japanese camp on the island of Borneo. The ambassador is none other than the commander of the Japanese camp. As Jesse skims the article, he sees that the ambassador will be visiting New York City. At that point, Jesse remembers growing up in New York City, and he knows the area where the ambassador and the president will be meeting to address the public. Jesse has a flashback of his promise to Shu that he would kill the commander if he ever got the chance.

Jesse tells Carla that he must make a trip back east, explaining that it has to do with bringing Jenny and Addi to America. He sneaks upstairs in the old ranch house and retrieves the old WWI rifle from its hiding spot along with a box of old ammunition. He can't let Carla see that he is taking the rifle with him to New York, so he wraps the rifle in a blanket and stashes it behind the truck seat. He puts the ammunition in his pack and takes off for New York.

Arriving in New York, Jesse begins to remember and recognize his old stomping grounds. He drives around slowly, looking for a vantage point where he will be able to view the Japanese diplomat. At last, he finds it, an abandoned warehouse directly across from where the diplomat will be meeting with the president. He carefully parks the pickup out of sight and takes his rifle and pack to an upstairs room in the warehouse.

Here, he will wait patiently and take his shot, but he won't have to wait long, because the appearance will be at noon. Jesse reaches into his pack and pulls out a deck of playing cards. He removes the black aces and black eights and pins them on the wall. Then he uses his pack as a pillow and takes a little nap. He is awakened by the bustle on the streets below. A crowd has gathered to get a look at the president and the Japanese diplomat. Jesse rechecks his rifle to make sure the magazine is full, and the chamber has a round in it. He pulls the cartridge from the magazine, holds it up to the light from the window, and says, "This is for you, Shu, wherever you may be."

The president and the diplomat step out on the stage to the cheers of the crowd. The president introduces him, and the diplomat takes the podium. Speaking in English, he begins to address the crowd. Jesse has opened the window just enough to get a good shot. Jesse takes careful aim and says, "It's an eye for an eye, asshole." Jesse squeezes the trigger, but the cartridge misfires with a loud click. Jesse reaches over with his left hand and chambers a second round, sending the misfired cartridge across the room.

As if he had actually heard the misfire, the diplomat pauses in midsentence and looks straight at the building where Jesse is positioned. Jesse can see him looking right at him, and he fires the shot, sending a fatal round right through the diplomat's eye.

"There you go, Shu," Jesse says out loud. "My debt is paid in full."

As the crowd screams in terror, Jesse makes his escape. He remembers his way around the city and will maintain as much stealth as he can while making his way back to the pickup that he has parked several blocks away. He tries his best to conceal the rifle that he does not want to leave behind, but a police officer catches a glimpse of him as he turns into an alley.

Jesse does not realize that he has been spotted and makes his way carefully down the alley toward his waiting vehicle.

The police officer summons additional officers to assist him, but is in no hurry to pursue the shooter, because the officer knows that the alley is blocked, and the shooter is trapped.

Jesse reaches the end of the alley. He looks around puzzled and says to himself, "Damn, this wasn't like this before, or else I'm not where I'm supposed to be." Believing that he had made a clean escape, Jesse starts back out of the alley, but is met by an overwhelming number of police officers and must surrender.

Jesse lays down his rifle and pack, and the police officers take him into custody. The secret service and FBI officers are waiting at the alley entrance as the police bring Jesse out. He is handed over to the federal officers.

As Jesse is taken away by the federal officers, his rifle and pack are turned over to a team of federal investigators who have been summoned to collect evidence from the place of the assassination and to sift through Jesse belongings. Among the team of investigators is the president's chief advisor, David McLain.

McLain and the other officers make their way to the room where the shooter fired his rifle. There is much chaos in the room, with officers taking photographs, officers examining the rifle and placing it in the open window to check the view for the shot.

There are other officers going through Jesse's pack for any documents that might provide identification or a motive for the shooting. While all this is going on, McLain is looking around and notices a shiny object lying on the floor across the room. Unnoticed, McLain walks slowly over to the object. He sees that it is an unfired cartridge. He looks around to make sure that no one is watching him, and he bends down, picking up the cartridge with his handkerchief. He places the cartridge in his pocket and walks back across the room.

Back in Australia, Jenny is watching as breaking news comes on, announcing the assassination of the Japanese diplomat in the United States. Jenny sits down to watch as it is announced that the shooter has been captured and identified as an Australian whose name is Erich Blanton. Jenny begins to cry. She places her hands over her face and whispers, "My god, Erich, what have you done?"

CHAPTER 13

WHITEHOUSE PLAN

A Remington pen-and-ink drawing is hanging on the wall of the Oval Office. There is a playing card stuffed in the corner of the frame. It is an old card, and the queen of diamonds is barely visible. Indeed, Jack, the captain of the downed aircraft on the island of Borneo, is the president of the United States.

The president is pacing the floor. The report from the assassination is on his desk, and he has read it. He goes to the door and summons his secretary, Jaime Smith, "Jaime, where the hell is McLain?"

"He is on his way, Mr. President," Jaime answers. "Mr. President, I have several phone messages here for you. Would you like them now? Some of them are very important. They are from the leaders of Japan and Australia, as well as others."

"I don't want to talk to anyone until I talk to McLain. He said it was important. Send him in the minute he arrives," the president snaps and closes the door.

While waiting for McLain to arrive, the president reviews the file for a second time, making note that according to documents found in the shooter's possession, the assassin is a man named Erich Blanton, an Australian visiting the United States on an Australian passport. The president knows that there have been ill feelings between the Australians and the Japanese ever since the war.

David McLain enters the president's office holding a package in his hand.

"Well, it's about time, McLain," the president states, "so what do you have? It is something good. The entire world is watching us right now, and I have to figure out how to deal with an Australian assassin."

"Perhaps not, Jack," David answers.

"What do you mean, David?" Jack asks.

"I realize," David begins, "that the investigators found information that led everyone to believe that the shooter was an Australian, but I don't believe that is really the case."

"And just who do you think he is?" Jack questions.

"Mr. President," David says seriously, "in the room where the shooting took place, I found an unspent cartridge which I had examined. The fingerprint on the cartridge indicates that the shooter is actually an American soldier."

"So, what other information do you have about this soldier?" Jack queries.

David begins again, "It would appear that this particular soldier was a sniper. However, it seems that he was killed prior to the US getting into the war. He was, though, somehow awarded the Medal of Honor. According to his record, which is quite vague, he risked his life to save a downed pilot. The record does not say where this all took place. The only other information contained in his file is that he was from some small town in Wyoming that no one has ever heard of."

The president gets a blank stare as the scene with Jesse telling him where he was from enters his mind. The president speaks out loud, "Barnum. Barnum, Wyoming, and he has a tattoo of two black aces and two black eights on his left chest area."

Jack turns and looks at the Remington drawing on his wall.

"That would explain the aces and eights tacked to the wall where the shooter was, but, Jack," David asks with a puzzled look, "how do you know about the tattoo and the small Wyoming town?"

Jack turns to David and says, "Because it was my life that he rescued. I was the downed pilot. We were on the island of Borneo, and neither of us was supposed to be there. That's why most of his record is purged. I am telling you right now, David, I want nothing to happen to this man. I left him behind once, and I am not going to do it again."

"The picture," David responds,

"I get it now, but why the queen of diamonds and not aces and eights?"

"He gave me that card when I had to wait alone for the rescue team," Jack says boldly. "He said his mother gave it to him to keep him safe and that it would keep me safe until the team arrived. But it wasn't the card. It was him who kept me safe. I thought that he had been killed holding off the Japanese. I am ashamed we did not go back and look for him. I am telling you right now to come up with some way to save this soldier!"

"I'll do what I can, Jack," David responds timidly, "but if this man is let go, we could have a world crisis on our hands. I'm talking a major international incident. As it stands right now, the Japanese want him released to them, and the Australians want him returned to Australia. God only knows what sides the other countries will take in all of this. Jack, we are talking about the assassination of a diplomat on American soil. This whole thing is going to get a lot of attention. To make matters even worse, he has a wife and daughter in Australia. They will be bombarded with news media. Hell, they won't be able to leave their house."

Jack turns back to the drawing and says softly, "Just do whatever it takes, David."

"I've had easier assignments," David mutters to himself as he leaves the Oval Office.

Jack walks over to the door and summons his secretary, "Jaime, I want you to get Bill Coe in here."

"Bill Coe the director of the CIA?" Jaime questions.

"Yes," Jack responds sarcastically, "do you know any other Bill Coe?"

Bill arrives at the Oval Office and asks as he walks in, "What is it that I can do for you, Mr. President?"

Jack looks up from his desk and says, "I'm sure that you are aware of the little crisis we have going on with this assassination of the Japanese diplomat. Well, as it turns out, the shooter is not who everyone thinks he is. He is an American soldier. He has a wife and daughter in Australia.

Your mission is a simple one. I want you to get them out of Australia and bring them here to the United States. Easy enough."

Bill looks at Jack, quite puzzled, and asks, "How can you know that? We at the CIA do not have that information. Where did your information come from?"

Jack responds, "How I got my information is not important. What is important is that the information I have is correct. Now I have asked you to do one simple thing. Can you just simply handle it?"

"Of course," Bill answers, "but it is going to take some planning."

"Just get it done as quickly as you can and let me know once the mission is completed," Jack demands.

Bill nods his head and leaves the Oval Office.

Time seems to drag on for Jack as he waits to hear from both Bill Coe and David McLain. Thoughts go through his mind as to the handling of the situation. He gets flashbacks of being downed on the island and being rescued by the lone soldier. He becomes even more adamant that he will not see him harmed in any way. He must be released unharmed to live out his life in peace.

Bill Coe returns to the Oval Office to report to the president. As he enters the office, he begins, "The mission has been accomplished as you wished, Mr. President."

"Very good, Bill," Jack states, "so where are they at this point in time, and what have you told them of this situation?"

"Of course, they have not been told anything other than we were intervening for their own protection," Bill tells Jack. "We have them in a safe house and will keep them there pending your orders."

"Very good," Jacks says. "I will send McLain to get together with you so that he can meet with them. Okay, that will be all for now. See that they are well taken care of."

"May I ask why you are so involved in this, Mr. President?" Bill asks.

"No," Jack responds sharply.

"Okay," Bill whispers as he leaves the Oval Office.

Very little time passes, and McLain shows up at the Oval Office carrying a briefcase.

"So do we have a plan, McLain?" Jack asks.

"Yes, Jack," David responds, "and we are ready to move forward."

"Wonderful," Jack says happily, "so let's go over the plan."

"With all due respect, Mr. President," David replies sheepishly, "I think it would be best if you didn't know the details of the plan. We really need to minimize your involvement here, and I will be the fall guy if word of this ever gets out. There is no need to jeopardize your presidency, sir."

"I appreciate your concern, David," Jack states, "but I want to know every detail and where you think the plan needs some additional backing. I want this to go smoothly and without a hitch. Every mind is important in this matter. Also, have you talked to the soldier's wife yet?"

"No," David replies, "I wanted to wait until I met with you, and we could discuss just exactly what I am to tell her. I didn't know you were going to bring her to the US, so I really don't know what your plan is at this point. I think it is best if we discuss it. Then I will relay the information to her so that she can be at ease."

"All right, David, all right," Jack concedes, "I guess I did leave you out of the loop on that one, but I needed you to concentrate on a plan to rescue the soldier. I didn't want you to worry about the wife and daughter situation until later. I was sure Bill Coe would be able to pull this one off without too much trouble. So, let's just put that behind us for now and let's take a look at the plan."

Reluctantly, David sets down his briefcase, opens it, and pulls out a large envelope. As he hands the envelope to Jack, he says, "Well, this is it. The best plan we could come up with."

As David is talking, Jack is opening the envelope. He pulls out a folder with the inscription on the front, "OPERATION DELAYED DEPARTURE."

"So," Jack asks, "there is a code name for this mission?"

"Yes, Jack," David replies, "we need to keep as tight a wrap on this as we possibly can. Very few people will actually know what we are doing. The fewer, the better."

"And the soldier?" Jack questions. "Will the soldier be advised as to what is going on?"

"We have no way of getting the information to him, Jack," David explains. "He is under constant surveillance. Anyone coming or going from his cell is watched and listened to."

"So, you are just going to allow him to believe that he will be receiving the death penalty?" Jack again asks.

"Well, Jack," David replies, "we haven't actually discussed what to tell the soldier or how to try and get information to him. We can't afford to compromise this mission by trying to inform the soldier."

"And you couldn't figure anything out?" Jack angrily asks. "Let's take a look at what you have for a plan, and then we will take care of the loose ends. Both the soldier and his wife need to know that absolutely nothing bad is going to happen to either of them. Do I make myself clear?"

"Yes, Mr. President," David replies.

Jack opens the folder marked "OPERATION DELAYED DEPARTURE" and asks David, "Why this code name for this operation?"

"Because, Jack," David replies, "we are going to delay his death by faking the execution."

"The whole world is going to be watching, and your plan is to fake the execution?" Jack demands to know.

"It is the only viable way to get the soldier out of this situation without causing an international uproar," David tells the president. "Let's go over the plan and then you can give it a thumbs up or down."

"Very well, David," Jack says and opens the folder to review the plan's details. While David waits silently, Jack goes over every detail of the operation. Finally, he looks up from his desk and says to David, "I like it. I like it a lot. Damn, I hope it works. This will put everyone in the clear and circumvent any major international problems. But we still need to let the soldier know that no harm is going to happen to him. Perhaps I should go and meet with him myself."

"As I have already said, Mr. President," David asserts, "telling the soldier our plan is not possible. The other thing is, until this whole thing is over and successfully completed, I feel that it is best that the soldier does not know that the president is involved. Should something go wrong, and this thing blows up on us, it will be best if we can deny that the president had any knowledge of this operation."

"David," Jack scoffs, "you of all people should know that nothing is impossible. You have a great plan here, but perhaps you are right. Yes, keeping me out of all this may be best after all. I just hate not letting the soldier know something." The president turns to the drawing on the wall, scratches his head, and turns back to David. "I've got it!" Jack exclaims. Then reaching into his desk drawer, he pulls out two decks of cards and opens both decks. Jack spreads out one deck very carefully so as not to disturb the order of the cards. From the other deck, he removes the queen of diamonds and exchanges it with the queen of hearts in the first deck. He then gathers the cards up and places them back in their container. Handing the deck to David, Jack says, "Here, David, have Jaime reseal this deck of cards, then take them to the soldier. Eventually he will see the second queen of diamonds, and it will alert him that there is a plan."

"But what if the guard examines the cards and discovers the two queens?" David asks.

"That, David, is for you to see that it doesn't happen," Jack replies.

David shakes his head and takes the cards out to Jaime for resealing and then heads toward the prison where the soldier is being held.

CHAPTER 14

COMMENCE OPERATIONS

As David is arriving at the prison, the Whitehouse is releasing a statement that the Australian assassin is actually a US soldier and not Australian at all. Having never been officially discharged from the army, the soldier will stand a military court-martial for his crime. This of course, outrages the Australians, who demand proof of the American claim. The Japanese are pleased and believe that there will be no question of a guilty verdict, which will result in the death penalty for the assassin. However, Japan does not totally trust the United States and will be making plans of their own should things not go according to their wishes.

David enters the prison with the cards for the soldier. He is stopped prior to his entry into the prisoner's cell, and the guard asks, "What is your business here today?"

"I am here to visit with the prisoner and inform him that his true identity has been discovered. He will stand a military court-martial, be found guilty, and face a lethal injection," David informs the guard.

"I need to do a pat down prior to letting you in," the guard explains.

"Very well," David responds.

The guard is quite thorough as he is examining David, and in the process of his search, he discovers the deck of cards in David's jacket pocket. He pulls the deck of cards out and holding them in front of David, says, "You are very lucky, mister. I first thought that this was a weapon of some type. Just what are the cards for?"

David, pretending to be embarrassed, answers, "I am truly sorry. I had actually forgotten that they were there. I was in a meeting with the president, and he gave me the deck of cards. You can see right there that the deck has the seal of the president of the United States," David says, pointing to the seal on the deck of cards.

"They will have to remain here with me until you come out," the guard states firmly.

"Oh, I have no use for them. I am much too busy for card games," David replies. "Perhaps I can give them to the prisoner. Surely, he has time for card playing."

"I will have to look the cards over," the guard implies. "Why don't you just leave them with me if you don't want them?" he questions jokingly.

"I will bring you a deck the next time I visit," David tells the guard.

"Very well," the guard answers as he opens the deck of cards and looks through them. Placing the cards back in their box and handing them to David, the guard says, "I guess they are fine. Go ahead, and you can leave the cards with the prisoner." The guard then opens the gate to the soldier's cell.

The days pass slowly for Jesse, with nothing more to do while awaiting his fate than to play solitaire. Jesse notices that in all his games, he has never been able to play the queen of hearts, and during this game, he finds that although he has already played the queen of diamonds, he has just turned up a second queen of diamonds. He gathers all the cards up and begins to sort them out. Sure enough, there is no queen of hearts, but there are two queens of diamonds. Jesse thinks back in his mind to the time his mother gave him the queen of diamonds to keep him safe. Then he remembers giving that card to the injured pilot. Jesse realizes that this must be some covert sign to let him know that everything is going to be all right. But who could know about the queen of diamonds other than the pilot? Is the pilot somehow involved with this scheme? Jesse will wait and see what transpires.

Jesse is given a military court-martial and sentenced to be put to death by lethal injection. The sentence is to be carried out within thirty days. Jesse requests to contact his wife and child in Australia but is unable to get in contact with her. In lieu of contacting his wife, Jesse contacts Mick Reichle, who informs him that his wife and child have disappeared. Jesse continues to realize that something is going on. He picks up the deck of cards and takes both queens of diamonds out of the deck. Looking at the queens, he whispers to himself, "I may need both of you to watch over me this time." He then places one queen in each of his shirt pockets.

As the execution draws near, a guard delivering lunch to Jesse remarks, "Well, buddy, you must be a real important guy. According to today's paper, there is going to be an entire delegation of Japanese dignitaries here to witness your execution."

"Why am I not surprised?" Jesse remarks.

Scenarios continue to wander through Jesse's mind as to what is going on. He believes that somehow, the pilot has intervened, or at the very least he has caused some sort of intervention. Things just aren't adding up, though—the two queens, his wife and daughter missing, the execution moving forward with no word of a pardon of any kind. Jesse places his hands over his face and says to himself, "Okay, big guy, I believe you know what is going on, and I sure hope that whatever it is, everything turns out alright."

The Japanese delegation is seated as Jesse is led into the room for the lethal injection. They can see him, but he cannot see them. As he looks around the room at the guards, he cannot find a friendly face anywhere, and he begins to doubt himself about the intervention. He has the queens nestled in his shirt pockets, and he pats each one before he is laid down and strapped onto the execution bed. When asked if he has any last words, Jesse looks directly at the one-way window and says boldly, "I did it for Shu!" The IVs are hooked up, and outside the window there is total silence. The guards and the doctor leave the room and make ready for the injection. The clock has only thirty seconds until it is time, and it clicks one second at a time very slowly. The telephone near the doctor hangs silent. The clock strikes the final second, and the doctor begins the injection. Jesse has a flashback to the time his mother was leaving him at the orphanage. He wants to go with her. He begs and begs, but she tells him he cannot go where she is going. He must stay here because it is not his time. Jesse slowly falls into a coma, and in a matter of only a few minutes, Jesse James is dead.

The Japanese witnesses stand as the doctor enters the room where the lifeless body lies. He checks for a pulse and listens for a heartbeat.

There being none, the doctor declares Jesse dead, pulls a sheet over Jesse's head, and leaves the room as the lights go out.

The guard in the room with the Japanese delegation announces that the lethal injection has been completed and the prisoner is deceased.

"One moment please," one of the Japanese delegates demands, "we have our own doctor here with us, and we want our doctor to examine the body."

"That is totally out of the ordinary," the guard explains. "I will have to contact my superior to find out if that will be possible." The guard goes to the phone and speaks with the administering doctor. He explains that the Japanese want to have their own doctor examine the body.

"I will be out in just a minute to speak to them," the doctor responds. He then whispers to himself, "That is not part of the plan. Surely, their doctor will be able to detect the faint heartbeat. But I can't stall them, the injection will wear off within thirty minutes, and this plan will fail miserably."

The doctor walks out and introduces himself. He says to the delegation, "I understand you would like to examine the body. Is that correct?"

"Yes," the delegation leader responds, "we have our own doctor, and we want him to examine the body. Please, will you show him the way?"

"But of course," the doctor answers hesitantly, "right this way."

The Japanese doctor prepares to examine the body. He first checks for a pulse and then opens Jesse's shirt to listen for a heartbeat. He looks closely at the two black aces and two black eights tattooed on Jesse's chest. He shows no emotion as he hears the faint beat. Then he listens again. Yes, indeed there is a heartbeat.

The doctor watches closely but cannot tell if the Japanese doctor has heard the heartbeat or not. Time is passing quickly, and he is afraid Jesse may begin to stir.

The Japanese doctor looks out the window and nods his head. The assassin is dead. The rest of the Japanese bow to one another and prepare to depart. Blocking the view from the Japanese delegation, the Japanese doctor reaches into his bag and places something into Jesse's hand. He closes Jesse's hand tight so the item will not fall out. Then the Japanese doctor looks over at the American doctor and nods, asking, "Is there a place to wash up now?"

"Right this way," the doctor states and ushers the Japanese doctor out of the execution room, closes the curtain over the window, and turns off the light.

The Japanese doctor pulls up his sleeves to wash up, revealing the cigarette burns and the crossed swords tattoo. He washes up, dries his hands, and thanks the doctor for allowing his examination.

As the Japanese doctor begins to leave, the American doctor states, "I don't believe I caught your name, Doctor."

"I don't believe it was ever given," the Japanese doctor answers. "I am Dr. Shu."

The Japanese delegation leaves, and the doctor hurries back to Jesse. Waiting in the shadows is David McLain. David shows himself as the doctor walks in. "That was close," David tells the doctor as he helps place Jesse on a transport table. The doctor nods in agreement, and Jesse begins to stir.

"Be still, son," the doctor says to Jesse. "We are not out of danger yet. Please be as still as you possibly can."

David and the doctor take Jesse into the morgue, where a change of clothes and documents are waiting for him. The doctor pulls the sheet off Jesse. They wait for Jesse to fully recover so David can explain everything to him. Very dreary from the injection, Jesse opens his hand and metal objects fall to the floor. David picks them up and looks at them. They are Jesse's dog tags from the island of Borneo.

"Where did these come from?" David asks the doctor.

"The Japanese doctor," the doctor begins. "I thought I saw him put something in Jesse's hand, but I didn't want to waste any time questioning him. Why do you suppose he did it, and how is it that he had Jesse's dog tags?"

"My dog tags, did you say?" Jesse questions as he is trying to wake up.

"Why yes, Jesse," David answers, handing the tags to Jesse.

"The Japanese boy on the island of Borneo had them," Jesse tells, David.

"Was the boy's name Shu?" David asks. "That was the name you gave in your last words."

"Yes, Shu," Jesse responds. "We made a pact, a promise to each other. I told him that if I got the chance, I would kill the commander for him. He was abused by the commander. He promised me that if he ever got the chance, he would help me escape. But how could the Japanese doctor have gotten the dog tags?"

"I believe I can answer that," the doctor states. "Did this Shu have burnt marks and a crossed swords tattoo on his right forearm?"

"Why yes," Jesse answers. "The crossed swords were an ownership tattoo that the commander branded him with, and he would put out his cigarettes on his arm."

"The Japanese doctor had just such marks," the doctor tells Jesse, "And he said his name was Dr. Shu."

"The diplomat," Jesse tells David and the doctor, "he was the commander on the island of Borneo. I recognized him in the newspaper when it was announced that he was coming to the US to meet with the president."

"Well," the doctor tells Jesse, "I believe that you have both kept your promises to each other. I couldn't understand why Dr. Shu didn't hear a faint heartbeat, but now I believe I know."

"Jesse," David begins, "I can't possibly explain everything right now. We must hurry. I have clothes here for you. You must change so we can be on our way. I also have documents here for you. I am afraid we have to change your identity so the Japanese will never find out that they have been duped. Here, go change now, and I will explain everything as we go on our way."

Jesse has been given a new identity; he is now C. Wyatt Drury. David explains to Jesse that he is taking him to be reunited with his wife and daughter, and then they will be given passage back to Wyoming.

"Why are you doing all of this?" Jesse questions David.

"You are an American hero," David explains. "You earned the Medal of Honor. We don't leave our heroes behind."

Jesse looks at David quite puzzled, and David responds, "You didn't know you won the Medal of Honor, did you? Well, you have, it was given to your parents when it was thought that you were killed, and now you are going to be reunited with your family and will be able to live in peace on your ranch in Wyoming. We have contacted your family, and they will be expecting you."

"I can't wait to get back home," Jesse says.

Jesse is back home in Wyoming, where he is now known as C. Wyatt Drury; his wife Jenny Drury and their daughter Addi Drury are with him. All information in his records of Jesse James and Erich Blanton has been purged. Those people no longer exist, and as far as the Japanese are concerned, the assassin has been executed.

C. Wyatt is out working cattle in a pasture near the house when he looks around and notices a group of black cars traveling along the road toward his house. He immediately stops what he is doing and makes his way back home as he feels that something may be wrong.

When he arrives at the ranch house, C. Wyatt can see that one of the cars has the presidential seal on the side. He gets off his horse, ties it to the rail, and walks over to a man standing guard at the car.

"What is going on here?" C. Wyatt asks.

Reaching around to open the car door, the guard tells C. Wyatt, "The President of the United States is here to see you."

"Why?" C. Wyatt asks.

As the president exits the car, the guard tells C. Wyatt, "He will explain everything to you."

The president reaches out to shake hands with C. Wyatt and says, "C. Wyatt Drury, is that correct?"

"Yes," C. Wyatt responds, shaking the president's hand, "but why are you here?"

"I believe I have a few items of yours that will help me to explain everything," the president says as he walks around to the back of the car. He reaches into the trunk and retrieves the old WWI rifle. He hands it to C. Wyatt and says, "I believe this is yours."

"Why, yes," C. Wyatt answers, "but why is the president of the United States returning this to me? It could have been shipped to me, and actually, I thought it had been destroyed."

"For the record," the president begins reaching into his pocket, "it has been destroyed. I also have this," the president says, handing C. Wyatt the old queen of diamonds.

"My good luck card," C. Wyatt says, puzzled. "Where did you… how did you get this?"

"You gave it to me," the president answers. "My name is Jack, and at that time your name was Jesse. I was the pilot on the island of Borneo, and you gave me the card to keep me safe. I guess it worked. I guess it worked for both of us."

"Jack?" C. Wyatt questions as the president nods his head. "So that explains the second queen of diamonds in the presidential deck of cards."

"Exactly," Jack tells C. Wyatt. "We had no other way to let you know that everything was going to be all right. I hope you were able to pick up on the hint."

"I didn't exactly know for sure," C. Wyatt tells Jack, "But I knew something was up."

"Good," Jack says, "there is one other thing. Would you please turn around and face your mother, wife, and daughter?" C. Wyatt does as the president asks.

Jack opens a box with a Medal of Honor in it. He takes it out and places it around C. Wyatt's neck, saying, "I wanted the honor of presenting this to you in person. You are an American hero. You risked your life to save mine, and I went on to become the president of the United States, partially inspired by a certain drawing that I saw in the Phoenix Art Museum. Here, I want you to have that also." C. Wyatt turns around and Jack hands him the drawing of *They Left Him Thar in the Trail*, and Jack says, "I bought it for you."

"I don't know what to say," C. Wyatt says.

"There is nothing to say," Jack tells C. Wyatt. "May you live out the rest of your life in peace. I thank you for all that you have done. God bless you."

The president shakes C. Wyatt's hand one more time, gets into his car, and they all drive away.

A report is made to the Japanese military commander that it appears that the execution was successful, although there was one thing in question. The prisoner made a remark just prior to his injection that he did it for Shu. Dr. Shu was the examining doctor that went to witness the execution with the delegation. It now appears that our Dr. Shu was a slave boy of the diplomat when he was the commander on the island of Borneo.

The commander summons Dr. Shu.

Being told that the commander wants to question him about the execution, Dr. Shu commits suicide by injecting himself with poison, and he leaves the following note behind:

> I, Dr. Shu, have betrayed my country, an act that I deeply regret. I had hoped that it would never be discovered. The prisoner that was to be executed was an imprisoned American soldier while I was on the island of Borneo with the diplomat. He was the commander of the camp and tortured both the American soldier and myself. The soldier and I made a promise to each other that he would kill the commander for me if he ever got the chance, an act which he carried out. I made him a promise that if I ever

got the chance, I would help him escape. The opportunity to make good on my word came at the execution.

I knew who he was from the aces and eights that he had tattooed on his chest. I did hear a faint heartbeat, but could not bring myself to report it, and so I declared him dead. America has duped Japan, and unfortunately, I have taken part in it. I sincerely apologize to my country for my actions. It was not my intent to bring disgrace upon myself or my country.

Signed, Dr. Shu

Doctor Shu's note, along with the report of his death, is delivered to the commander. There is also a report from the Japanese intelligence agency that not only was the execution not carried out, but that the president of the United States was the pilot who crashed on the island of Borneo and escaped. Surely, the president was part of the facade. The commander is outraged and calls in his military advisors. Addressing his advisors, he says, "It would appear that we have been duped by the Americans. I want you to send them a message so they will know that we know."

C. Wyatt and his family are all settled in and enjoying life on the ranch. One day, Addi goes to her daddy and asks, "Will you teach me how to shoot, Daddy?"

"Well sure, Addi," C. Wyatt responds. "Let's get something to shoot with."

C. Wyatt gets a rifle, but before letting Addi shoot, he says, "Well, before we shoot, we need to see which eye is your shooting eye. Here now, hold up one finger and look at that fence post with both eyes open. Then close one eye, open it, and close the other eye. One eye will keep the finger on the post, and the other will move it off. The one that keeps it on the post is your shooting eye."

Addi does as her father says and then tells him, "I guess it's my left eye. That's the one that keeps it on the post."

"I'm not surprised," C. Wyatt says, patting Addi on the back. "Let's go shooting."

While Addi and C. Wyatt are out practicing shooting, Jenny and Carla are watching TV. A news break comes on the television reporting that the president has been shot in Dallas, Texas, and has been rushed to the hospital. "Oh my god, no," Jenny exclaims and rushes out the door to relay the news to C. Wyatt.

"Wyatt," Jenny calls, "you must come quickly. The president has been shot."

They all hurry back to the house and quietly wait for news on the president's condition. It is announced that the president is dead.

The next morning, as C. Wyatt is out doing chores, he hears a helicopter in the distance. The sound gets closer and closer until finally he sees it. The helicopter circles and then lands in the pasture. As C. Wyatt approaches the helicopter, a three-star general gets out and greets him by simply saying, "Your country needs you."

www.ingramcontent.com/pod-product-compliance
Lightning Source LLC
LaVergne TN
LVHW040155080526
838202LV00042B/3170